PAIRING A DECEPTION

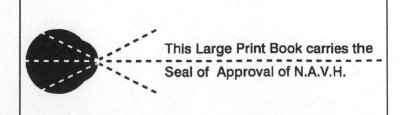

A SOMMELIER MYSTERY

PAIRING A DECEPTION

NADINE NETTMANN

WHEELER PUBLISHING
A part of Gale, a Cengage Company

Farmington Hills, Mich • San Francisco • New York • Waterville, Maine
Meriden, Conn • Mason, Ohio • Chicago

GALE
A Cengage Company

LIBRARY OF CONGRESS CIP DATA ON FILE.
CATALOGUING IN PUBLICATION FOR THIS BOOK
IS AVAILABLE FROM THE LIBRARY OF CONGRESS

ISBN-13: 978-1-4328-5454-6 (softcover)

Published in 2018 by arrangement with Midnight Ink, an imprint of Llewellyn Publication, Woodbury, MN 55125-2989 USA

Printed in Mexico
1 2 3 4 5 6 7 22 21 20 19 18

To the counties of Napa, Sonoma, Mendocino, Santa Barbara, and everyone affected by the California wildfires.
My heart is with you.

ACKNOWLEDGMENTS

My sincere appreciation to Terri Bischoff, Danielle Burby, Nicole Nugent, and the entire team at Midnight Ink. Thank you to Kevin Brown and Pierre Droal for another stunning cover.

Thank you to Melanie Hooyenga and Sara Spock for your feedback as well as support and camaraderie. Thank you to Solomon Mangolini for your excellent notes, Irene Phakeovilay for checking my details, and Christine Zahka for proofreading. A special thank you to Kelsey Hertig and Amy Scher.

Thank you to my critique group: Gretchen McNeil, Jennifer Wolfe, Julia Shahin Collard, James Matlack Raney, and Brad Gottfred.

Thank you to my parents for your encouragement and my mom for reading this manuscript multiple times. A heartfelt thank you to my husband, Matthew, for your unwavering support.

7

And to all of my readers, I raise a glass of wine to you and thank you for reading. Cheers!

CHAPTER PAIRING
SUGGESTIONS

One: Sparkling Rosé — Santa Barbara, California

Two: Cava — Penedès, Spain

Three: Zinfandel — Lodi, California

Four: Sauvignon Blanc — Napa Valley, California

Five: Crémant de Limoux — Languedoc, France

Six: Gewürztraminer — Monterey, California

Seven: Barbera d'Alba — Piedmont, Italy

Eight: Grauburgunder — Pfalz, Germany

Nine: Viognier — Central Coast, California

Ten: Mencía — Bierzo, Spain

Eleven: Aglianico — Campania, Italy

Twelve: Chenin Blanc — Stellenbosch, South Africa

Thirteen: Verdejo — Rueda, Spain

Fourteen: Beaujolais — Moulin-À-Vent, France

Fifteen: Sekt — Mosel, Germany

9

Sixteen: Chardonnay — Adelaide Hills, Australia

Seventeen: Pouilly-Fumé — Loire Valley, France

Eighteen: Pinot Noir — Casablanca Valley, Chile

Nineteen: Vermentino — Sardinia, Italy

Twenty: Chardonnay — Santa Barbara, California

Twenty-One: Zweigelt — Kremstal, Austria

Twenty-Two: Moscato d'Asti — Piedmont, Italy

Twenty-Three: Riesling — Finger Lakes, New York

Twenty-Four: Agiorgitiko — Nemea, Greece

Twenty-Five: Salice Salentino — Puglia, Italy

Twenty-Six: GSM Blend — Paso Robles, California

Twenty-Seven: Cabernet Franc — Bourgueil, France

Twenty-Eight: Cabernet Blend — Columbia Valley, Washington

Twenty-Nine: Pinot Noir — Central Otago, New Zealand

Thirty: Malbec — Cahors, France

Thirty-One: Super Tuscan — Tuscany, Italy

Thirty-Two: Syrah — Walla Walla, Washington

Thirty-Three: Bandol — Provence, France

Thirty-Four: Petit Verdot — Napa Valley, California

Thirty-Five: Tokaji Aszú — Tokaj, Hungary

Thirty-Six: Late Harvest Riesling — Columbia Valley, Washington

ONE:
PAIRING SUGGESTION:
SPARKLING ROSÉ —
SANTA BARBARA, CALIFORNIA

A refreshing wine, perfect for
the summer or early fall.

Wine and food festivals have a gentle hum
to them as they combine three great elements: wine, food, and people who love
both. The sound is a mixture of wine being
poured, chefs crafting their dishes, guests
chatting, and an overall excitement in the
air, carried through the tents or lawns where
they are held. These events happen all year
long and all over the country, but an added
bonus to those in the late summer or early
fall is the harvest season, when the grapes
reach the last stage of their growing cycle
and are plucked from the vines, on their
way to become wine. Guests often get a
glance of the activities and may even be able
to participate in them.

I stood at the edge of the lawn where the
Harvest Days Wine and Food Festival was

about to start. The four-day event at the New Sierra Hotel in Santa Ynez celebrated the wine regions of Santa Barbara, California. Located close to the ocean and backed by rolling hills, Santa Barbara wine country was known for its picturesque setting, a long grape-growing season, and the world-class wines created there, especially Pinot Noir, Chardonnay, and Rhône varietals. The region was also a little over two hours north of Los Angeles, where I grew up, not that I was going there. Not sure when I would again. As far as I knew, my father still didn't want to see me since my not-so-innocent past was revealed. It didn't matter that I had been law-abiding since that moment, but a cop's daughter wasn't supposed to break the law. The damage was done and I wasn't sure when, if ever, it would be repaired.

I shook the thought off as I stared at the two white tents in front of me. I couldn't hear the gentle hum. Not yet. Although the opening ceremonies were still about an hour away, the chefs would already be prepping the food and people would start lining up, ready to be the first ones in the tent.

Dean was dropping our bags off at the nearby Lancaster Hotel while I studied, and although the flash card app was open on my phone, I hadn't looked at it in the last few minutes. I needed to focus, and being near the festival wasn't helping. Even though I had studied the whole drive, I wanted to get a few more minutes in. My next test, the Advanced Sommelier exam and the third of four steps to Master Sommelier, was only a few days away. Not great timing for a wine and food festival, but I didn't want to miss this weekend and I figured I could use a brain break before the three-day exam.

I pulled open the wooden door of the Lancaster Hotel to find a quiet place to sit while I waited for Dean. A large stone fireplace stood in the middle of the lobby and dark wooden beams lined the whole hotel. The bar, located in the corner, had green leather chairs like it was from a time when the bartender would already know your name as well as your favorite drink. Even though I knew it was much smaller than the palatial New Sierra, which had ballrooms to hold the wine seminars, the cozy atmosphere and charm of this building gave me a calm and welcome feeling.

I took a seat on a couch in the corner of the lobby and looked at my phone, the bright red flashcard app on the screen.

"What are the ten Crus of Beaujolais?" I

paused for a moment as I thought about the region of France known for producing a lighter red wine from the Gamay grape. Each Cru had a distinct taste due to the soil, climate, location, and more. The vineyards within each Cru could label their wine with the Cru name, such as Saint-Amour, a popular wine for Valentine's Day. "Saint-Amour, Juliénas, Chénas, Moulin-à-Vent, Fleurie, Chiroubles, Morgon, Régnié, Côte de Brouilly, and Brouilly." I pressed the screen to flip the card over as I took a deep breath. I was correct and had named them in order from north to south.

I went to the next flashcard and read out the question. "What is the name of the aphid that nearly destroyed the wine industry in Europe? Phylloxera."

I paused before I hit the next screen. I still wasn't used to electronic flash cards. I enjoyed the paper ones, as I learned the facts while writing them, but my whole supply had been stolen earlier in the year. It was too much work to replace them and the test was coming up fast, so now I used the electronic ones. Still, it wasn't the same.

I glanced out the window to the white tents on the lawn. The hum of wine, food, and happy attendees would begin soon.

"There you are," said Dean as he approached. Even though he had driven most of the five-hour journey from San Francisco, he still looked refreshed and excited. "You have a strange expression. Everything okay? Or are you just going over wine facts in your head?"

"Do I do that?"

"You tell me."

"Sometimes." Though it was true — I often went through maps of regions or mentally recited the prestige cuvée of Champagne houses such as Taittinger's Comtes de Champagne and Louis Roederer's Cristal. Not to mention the ten Crus of Beaujolais were still going through my mind, especially Saint-Amour. It was a reminder that this was our first weekend away together.

I turned off the app and put my phone in my pocket.

"Done with studying?" Dean raised his eyebrows, his blue eyes staring at me as if I was doing something wrong.

"I need to let it all sink in. Are we set with everything here?"

"The bags have been put away and apparently festival passes can be picked up at the New Sierra Hotel."

I could sense a little nervousness in his voice. We had been dating for six months, but our different schedules — my working mostly evenings and weekends at Trentino Restaurant and Dean working rotating shifts as a Napa Valley detective — and the distance between Napa and San Francisco made time together difficult. Today was the start of four uninterrupted days together. "Great. Shall we walk over to the New Sierra?"

Dean shifted his feet and sat down on the couch next to me. "I'm sorry I didn't book us there. Maybe that would have been easier . . ." His voice fell away.

"No, I like this hotel." We had talked about it while planning and decided that we wouldn't mind the walk from the Lancaster to the event. "It's cozy and charming. Honestly, it's great." I smiled at him, but he kept a stoic expression. "Come on," I said. "It's going to be a great weekend. The festival will be a lot of fun."

He took a deep breath. "You'll keep studying, right? I don't want this, or me, to be a distraction from your test."

"You won't and the festival won't be, either. I'll still be studying, sipping wine while I go through my notes." But even as I said it, a little bit of concern crept into my mind. Not just anyone could take the Advanced. It required an application, an acceptance, and a three-day course prior to the exam, not to mention an extremely low pass rate. Friends had been on the waiting list for years, but after I took the course in Texas a few months ago, my application had gone through for the exam this week. If I failed, I wasn't sure when I would be able to take it again. I might be back on the wait list for another year or two.

Dean, as if he could read my thoughts, put his hand on my knee and squeezed. "You're going to do great. I'll help you study, too."

"Thanks, but I'm definitely ready for some wine and festivities. Shall we go get our passes?" I stood up.

"Yes," said Dean as he joined me.

"No, I have to stay here," shouted a woman near the front desk. "You have to find me a room." Her white dress barely hid her thin frame and her shoulder-length dark hair swayed with her movements.

"I'm sorry, ma'am, but we're all sold out. Perhaps you can try the New Sierra?"

"No, no!" She stomped her foot like a child who had just been told they can't have the piece of candy they want.

"There's nothing I can do, ma'am," replied the attendant.

The woman pounded her foot again on

the wood floor.

"Sounds like someone might need some wine," I whispered to Dean.

"Yes," he replied. "As well as a hotel room."

We walked past as the lady continued to argue. It wouldn't do any good. If the hotel was sold out, she could stomp her foot all she wanted, but it wouldn't magically make a room vacant.

Dean held open the door and the scent of freshly cut grass greeted us as we crossed the lawn.

I pointed to the smaller of the two tents. "I'm sure that's where they'll have the opening ceremonies today, and then the grand tasting on Sunday in the bigger tent. More people come to that one. Today's event will be small since it's only Thursday." I stared at the entrance, the red partition across it to stop people from entering. "I'm surprised attendees aren't lining up already."

"Why would they line up? Is there a benefit to being first?"

"I would say yes, so they can be the first ones to taste a dish, or so they don't worry about food running out in case the chefs didn't prepare enough for the entire group." I paused as another reason came to mind. "Or I guess so they can get food without waiting in line. If they're first in, they can choose any stand they want."

"So waiting in line, to avoid other lines?" said Dean with a smile.

I laughed. "It doesn't make sense but it does. There'll be lines the whole weekend, especially at the seminars so people can get a good seat."

Dean's phone beeped.

"Everything okay?"

"Just work," he said as he looked at it. "But it's fine."

"Are you sure you're okay taking time off for the festival?"

"One hundred percent. I'm excited to spend time with you and learn more about your world of wine. I've been looking forward to this for weeks." A strange smile appeared on his face, one that I wasn't sure I had seen before.

I stared at him. "What's going on?"

"I might have a little surprise for you on Saturday."

"What is it?"

"If I told you, it wouldn't be a surprise anymore." He winked but then turned serious. "It's wine-related."

I nudged him. "Spill it."

"You'll see. Patience."

"Patience is not one of my virtues," I replied.

"I'm aware," said Dean. "But you'll find out soon. You'll be happy, I promise."

We entered the expansive marble lobby of the New Sierra Hotel. Guests milled about, several already wearing green festival passes on lanyards around their necks. A coffee shop in the corner emitted the sound of fresh beans being ground.

The Harvest Days Wine and Food Festival took up the majority of the hotel and while attendees could purchase tickets to individual events, passes for the entire four-day festival were steep. Working for Paul Rafferty, a side job I did expanding his wine collection in addition to working at Trentino Restaurant as a sommelier, provided me with some much-needed extra cash but not enough to afford a festival pass. Fortunately, I secured one through Trentino as a pourer for the grand tasting on Sunday.

Dean joined me on a volunteer pass and the weekend had turned into a nice little getaway for the two of us.

"There we go," I said, motioning to a table on the far side with a sign for Harvest Days on the front. "Registration table."

Two ladies wearing identical Harvest Days Wine and Food Festival shirts, one in blue and one in green, sat behind the table. "Good afternoon," they said in unison as we approached.

"Are you already registered?" said the lady in green.

"Or would you like to purchase a pass?" added the lady in blue.

"Just checking in. My name is Katie Still-well."

"Katie Stillwell, Katie Stillwell," said the lady in green as she went down the list. "Ah, yes. You're pouring for us on Sunday."

"That's right." I smiled and saw that Dean was smiling, too. He had a proud look on his face, but all I was doing was pouring wine. Something I did every night at Trentino. Except at the restaurant, I was able to tell the story of the wine as I opened the bottle for the guests at the table. I had never worked at a wine and food festival before, but I had attended several of them and I knew there wouldn't be much time for conversation between pours. However, there might be a few guests who wanted to know, and that made me happy.

"Would you like to add additional events?" asked the lady in blue.

"We have special wine lunches and wine dinners," said the lady in green.

"With winemakers, too," they said in unison.

"No, thank you. There's enough main events that we'll be fine," I replied. I knew the special events would have a high price tag and I didn't want Dean to think he had to pay for those. He was already paying for the hotel.

"Here you go," said the lady in green as she handed me a badge that read KATIE STILLWELL, STAFF.

It was nice to know I was official. I put the lanyard around my neck and waited for the next badge, but the lady in green just continued to smile at me, as did the lady in blue.

I glanced at Dean and then back at the ladies. "There should be a second badge. I have a volunteer guest and was told there would be two." My lungs tightened as the lady in green looked at the list. If there wasn't a volunteer badge for Dean, the weekend would be ruined. When the festival director, Mr. Tinsley, invited me to pour for the event, he clearly said I was free to bring a guest to help volunteer. Maybe my email to him had gotten lost, or perhaps he forgot to add Dean to the list. There was no way Dean would want to pay the hefty amount for a weekend pass and if he couldn't go into the events with me, our weekend together would end up being a weekend apart. I tried to take a deep breath, but my lungs wouldn't expand.

The lady in blue reached over and pointed to a line on the list.

"Oh, that's right," said the lady in green. "Here's the note about a guest. My mistake." She flipped through the accordion folder as relief flooded through me. "Dean, correct?"

"Yes," replied Dean. "It might be under John Dean."

"Nope," the woman in blue said as she handed him a badge.

Dean stared at the badge, his eyebrows raised. A smile spread across his face followed by a deep laugh.

"What?" I asked.

He kept laughing.

I reached for his badge and he let it slide out of his hands. It said the Harvest Days Wine and Food Festival, just like mine, but then I noticed the name. It didn't say John Dean, or even just Dean. It said Dean Stillwell. My stomach dropped.

I looked up at him. "I'm so sorry. We can get it changed." I turned to the ladies, but Dean put his hand on my shoulder.

"No, it's fine," he said with a smile in his

voice. "It'll be fun." He took the badge and put the lanyard around his neck. "It's like I'm incognito."

"Dean, no. We can get this changed." We didn't even use the words *boyfriend* and *girlfriend* very freely, let alone something like this.

"Don't. I'm here as your guest and," he said as he pointed to the badge, "everyone will definitely know I'm with you."

I waited to see if he was really okay with this. He had a small grin on his face. Dean Stillwell. It finally started to make me smile.

"There we go," said Dean. "Now you're seeing the humor in this."

"Sort of." I paused. "Mr. Stillwell."

"Hey now. That's Detective Stillwell to you."

"Don't forget your schedule of events," said the lady in green as she held out two booklets. "The opening reception starts in the west tent at five o'clock. Ooh, that's in about ten minutes."

"The seminars are in the ballrooms," said the lady in blue.

"And Sunday's grand tasting event is in the east tent," added the lady in green.

"Thank you." I took the booklets and handed one to Dean.

"You're welcome," they replied in unison.

I looked at Dean. "Well, shall we head over and get in line?"

"A line to avoid other lines? Lead the way." He held the door open for me.

"Get ready, you're going to learn a lot about wine this weekend."

"I'm looking forward to it. What about you? Aside from your flash cards, of course."

"There's always something to learn. Always." Both about wine and people, I wanted to add. I stared out at the lawn as guests gathered near the tents. One of them looked just like the lady in the white dress who had stomped her foot at the front desk. First impressions could be deceiving. Sometimes wines needed a little time to breathe before they opened up and were ready to be enjoyed. Sometimes people did, too.

Two:
Pairing Suggestion:
Cava — Penedès, Spain

A sparkling wine similar to Champagne
and ideal for celebrations and festivities.

The lady was no longer in view when we reached the end of the line as it curved around the tent, away from the entrance.

"The schedule says it should start now," said Dean as he looked at the booklet. "They're running late."

"Maybe they want to make sure all of the chefs and wineries are ready." I glanced at my watch. "Hopefully they let people in soon." I hoped this wasn't a sign of things to come for the weekend.

Dean took out his phone, a serious look on his face.

"Work again? Is it still the Harper case?"

He had taken a few calls about the case on the drive down and as much as he tried to hide it, I knew work was still on his mind.

"No." He swiped the screen.

"Picture time?"

He shook his head. "What is the Méthode Champenoise?"

"Wait, what do you have there?" I tilted his phone so I could see it. The screen was full of the bright red flash card app. "You have my flash cards on here?"

"Just a few I found online. I know they're not yours, but I wanted to help you study."

I stared up at Dean, his blond hair moving in the breeze. The gesture surprised me. Even though the time I spent preparing for my exams put pressure on our relationship, he wanted to help me. "Thank you."

"What are you studying for?" asked the lady in front of us who had turned around. She was in her late forties with red hair that framed her face and bright green eyes surrounded by too much mascara. The festival lanyard competed for space with a sizeable white necklace that reminded me of Wilma Flintstone except her dress was blue.

"The Advanced Sommelier exam," I replied.

"What?"

"An exam about wine," I added.

"Oh." She nodded as she brushed her bangs away from her eyes. "I love wine."

I smiled. "Me, too."

29

She returned her focus to the line in front of her.

"So, what is the Méthode Champenoise?" repeated Dean. "Hopefully I'm saying that right."

"You pronounced it right. The traditional method for creating sparkling wine, where all the bubbles are actually produced inside the bottle."

Dean nodded. "Correct. What's the Charmat Method?"

The lady stepped forward.

"I think the line might be moving."

"Katie?"

"Sorry, we're at a festival and I think the event is about to start."

Dean's face shifted even with his stoic demeanor. "I know how much this test means to you. I want to make sure this weekend doesn't get in the way."

"Thank you. I really love that you're helping me, but I'm definitely ready to take a break from studying, at least for a few hours, and enjoy my time with you." I paused. "And the Charmat Method is also known as the tank method and is primarily used for Prosecco. It's where the second fermentation takes place in a tank and then is transferred into bottles."

Dean nodded as he put away his phone.

"Well done. You've got this."

"Two or three questions doesn't mean I'm going to pass the test," I replied. "It has a really high fail rate, but I'm going to try my best."

"I have no doubt."

The line moved and volunteers at the tent entrance handed out wineglasses.

"This is your only glass. Don't put it down 'cause it might be hard to get another one," said the volunteer as he gave one to each of us.

Dean looked at the glass in his hand. "Do we only taste one wine for this event?"

"Yes, you can only stick with one wine even though there are hundreds here. Choose carefully." I nudged him. "I'm kidding. You reuse the same glass."

"What about the leftover wine from each pour? Won't it affect the next wine?"

"Each time you want to taste a new one, the server will do a quick wash for you where they pour a small amount of wine in, swirl it around, and then dump it. Then they'll pour the actual wine sample for you." I smiled. "I love that you don't want to mix the flavors. You're becoming quite the connoisseur."

"I live in Napa and I'm dating a sommelier. I want to know as much about wine

31

as I can."

We stepped into the tent.

Tables lined the sides with notable chefs and local restaurants serving up small bites of lobster brioche, mini fish tacos, risotto, pasta, and then a dessert section with cake pops and chocolate mousse. Interspersed between the food tables were wine stands, ready to offer a tasting of their best product. They never poured full glasses of wine, only an ounce, much to the dismay of heavy drinkers who came to the festival to eat and drink as much as they could.

"Are you sure you don't need to pour today?"

"No, just Sunday." I glanced at the signs above each stand. "Today the representatives from the wineries are pouring. On Sunday it's a general selection, so they wanted sommeliers to pour."

"Do you know any of them?"

"I know Darius is supposed to be here, so we'll see. I think he's coming down early Sunday." Darius was a member of my tasting group and a fellow employee at Trentino.

Dean motioned to the tables. "Where would you like to start? You're in charge this weekend. I'm following your lead."

I grinned. "I could get used to this, being

in charge."

People milled about on the large stage in the center, clearly getting ready to make an announcement, and guests held their wineglasses as they stood in line at each of the food tables. Full or empty, the glasses would stay in their hands for the duration of the event.

"Mini fish tacos."

"Of course," replied Dean with a smile. "I should have guessed."

"No, a clear guess would have been pasta. I'm changing it up a bit. Keeping you on your toes."

"Don't keep me on my toes too much. I might fall." Dean said it with a laugh, but I could sense a serious tone underneath.

When we had our mini tacos covered with shredded cabbage and aioli, we headed to a nearby wine stand and had the representative pour us each a tasting of the Sauvignon Blanc. Sauvignon Blanc was an ideal wine to pair with any dish you might want to squeeze a lemon on.

"Are there tables?" asked Dean as he looked around.

"No. Probably a high top or two, but usually you just eat as you stand or walk around."

"How do we balance the plate and the wine?"

"Practice." I smiled. "You'll get it." I held up my glass. "Cheers."

"Cheers," replied Dean. "To our first weekend away. May it be a great one."

We clinked the glasses and I took a sip. The Sauvignon Blanc was nicely tart with lemon flavors and, as I suspected, paired perfectly with the fish tacos.

Dean continued to struggle on how to eat while holding wine. I nudged him and pointed to my plate. I held my glass of wine by the stem, snuggled between my pinky and ring finger, while the plate was between my pointer finger and thumb, leaving my right hand completely free to eat.

"Not my first rodeo," I commented.

"Clearly," said Dean, and he shifted his glass and plate to mimic mine.

"Welcome to the 2018 Harvest Days Wine and Food Festival!" a voice echoed throughout the tent. I glanced up at the stage. Standing at the podium was Hudson Wiley. He was revered in the wine community and passed the Master Sommelier Exam in his early twenties a few decades ago.

We placed our empty plates on the collection tray to the side of the tent and walked toward the stage, wineglasses still in hand.

"Do you know him?" asked Dean.

I nodded. "I mean, I know who he is. I've never met him." He was notorious for his incredible memory, his ability to identify a wine within seconds, and the rumored amount of time he spent on his hair, whose curls were always styled in perfect form with a lot of gel.

"We're glad you could join us for this grand celebration," Hudson continued. "It's going to be a fantastic weekend and I'm honored to be your emcee. If you know who I am, then you know I'm Master Sommelier Hudson Wiley. If you don't know me, then why not?"

The crowd laughed.

"That must be the pin you'll wear one day," whispered Dean, referencing Hudson's large red MS pin glinting in the lights. "But first the green one next week," he added.

"You remembered the color of the Advanced pin?" His attention to this detail surprised me.

"Of course. I remember everything about you."

"Who here likes wine?" asked Hudson, his hands up in the air to get a response.

The crowd roared.

"Who here likes food?"

The crowd roared again.

"Well, you're in the right place! We have a lot of great events lined up, and I hope you'll come and greet me throughout the festival. We might even have a surprise or two, but I'll keep those under wraps at the moment. I can't give everything away, it would spoil the fun." He paused after the last word, as if he wasn't exactly having fun himself. His expression quickly transformed into his game face to hide any emotion and he continued. "Please let our wonderful host, the New Sierra Hotel, know if you need anything, and above all, enjoy yourself." Hudson raised a glass of Champagne. "Cheers!"

"Cheers!" replied the crowd in unison.

Hudson stepped back from the podium and shook hands with a shorter gentleman in horn-rimmed glasses who stood nearby.

"Well, what food would you like to try next?" asked Dean. "I think I saw a pasta dish over there."

"Actually," I said as Hudson stepped down from the stage, "I'd like to meet Hudson before the festival gets too busy. I'm sure people will want to talk to him all weekend, but if we can meet him now . . . then we can relax and enjoy the festival."

"Of course," replied Dean. "Pasta can wait." His voice had a hint of disbelief. He knew I rarely turned down pasta.

Hudson's glass of Champagne had already been replaced by red wine when we reached him. People gathered around him and he beamed a smile with every hand he shook. He genuinely seemed to be a people person, or had at least perfected his game face to appear so.

"We still need to talk," said the woman in the white dress from the Lancaster lobby. She was in her mid-twenties with high cheekbones, skin that glowed like a health-care professional, and a toned frame that suggested she'd never eaten a carb in her life. She exuded a mix of confidence and urgency, and although she was at a wine festival, she didn't have a glass or plate of food in her hands. "You promised."

"Now's not the time. Later," said Hudson as he moved aside and shook hands with someone else.

"Seems to be a little tension there," said Dean.

"Yep," I replied. "Maybe she still didn't get a room."

"Perhaps she wants his."

"Dean."

"What?" He shrugged. "It's a valid comment."

The woman continued to hover a few feet

away, pushing her dark brown hair behind her shoulders, though some of the strands fell forward, too short to stay back. Her focus was only on Hudson as people circled around him.

"Want to get food and come back?" asked Dean. "This might take a while."

"He's the star of the festival — the crowds will only get worse as the majority of people arrive tomorrow. Let's wait one more minute."

Hudson finished shaking hands with the next person and I saw a gap. I took advantage of the opportunity and stepped forward. "Hudson Wiley." I put out my hand as my lungs slightly tightened. I wanted to pass the tests like he did. I wanted the pin he earned. I wanted the respect that he had. "My name is Katie Stillwell. It's a pleasure to meet you."

"The pleasure is all mine." His handshake was firm and he was one of those people who looked you directly in the eye as if you had his entire attention and not a line of people waiting behind you to talk to him.

I motioned to Dean. "This is John Dean."

"Welcome to Harvest Days," he replied as they shook hands. Hudson returned his focus to me and stared as he took a sip of his wine. "Katie Stillwell," he repeated. "I know that name."

The comment surprised me but I maintained my composure, my game face on. "I'm a sommelier at Trentino in San Francisco. Maybe you've dined there?"

"Perhaps," he said and sipped again. "But I know it from somewhere else."

The tone in his voice made me wonder if he had heard about me solving the case at Frontier Winery. Or the work I did for Paul Rafferty. Or the times I had been questioned by police and even arrested. Had my troubles with the law extended to the wine world as well? Would it affect my journey to Master Sommelier?

A gentleman came up to him and Hudson shook his hand before returning his attention to me. "Katie Stillwell," he repeated.

Dean shifted next to me. "Do you live in the Bay Area? Maybe you know her from up there."

"No, I'm over in Denver." Hudson paused as he rubbed his forehead with his pointer finger. "Sorry, I'm usually better than this. I must be a little rattled. Still, don't tell me."

Dean made eye contact with me and motioned to the tables of food. I could tell he was uncomfortable, though there was no reason to be. I glanced at Hudson's left hand. There was a gold band around his ring finger. But I didn't want to put strain on Dean. It was time to go.

"I don't think we've actually met before," I said. "But if you remember, let me know. It was nice to meet you." I moved to the side to let the next person talk to him.

"Yes." Hudson stared out across the crowd and then snapped his fingers. "Ah, I've got it. You're taking the Advanced Exam this week, right?"

I stepped back to my original position in front of him. "I am." My surprise was clearly reflected in my voice.

"That's where I've seen your name. On the list of applicants. I'm proctoring the exam."

A swarm of nerves shot through me. "I'll be seeing you on Tuesday in Arizona then," I managed to say with a smile, but I knew it didn't hide the tension.

"You will." Hudson finished his glass and someone handed him a fresh one filled with red wine. A perk of being the guest of honor at the festival, I was sure. "We almost had to cancel that exam as we didn't have a proctor due to some family emergencies. Fortunately, I'm able to fill in."

After all my studying and prep, the last thing I wanted to do was wait another few months to take the test.

"I'm glad you didn't have to cancel it," replied Dean, who seemed much more comfortable now that he knew how Hudson knew my name. "How many people are taking the exam?"

Hudson paused. "I think we have fifty-two this time around." He nodded toward me. "Are you ready for it?"

"I think so. I mean, I've studied a lot." I stopped, knowing I was already sounding unsure of myself. I stood up straighter. I still met with my blind tasting group twice a week at Trentino, I had thousands of flash cards, and I had spent every spare minute of the last year studying. "I'm ready," I replied, even though I knew the test was extremely difficult and many didn't pass the first time.

"Good, I look forward to seeing you there." He glanced around and made eye contact with the woman in white, who was still only a few feet away. She shifted her focus to me and gave a hopeful expression, as if she could use the moment to start talking to all three of us.

Hudson returned his attention to me. "I have to go meet some people . . ." He paused. "Then I'm hosting one of the seminars, but let's get drinks tonight. I don't like to stay at the main hotel for these

41

events. I'm over at the Lancaster."

"We are, too," I replied.

"Great, drinks in the bar later. See you both then." He glanced over his shoulder and disappeared into the crowd.

The lady smoothed out her white dress and stared at us as if she debated approaching. I didn't know what was going on with her and Hudson, but I knew I didn't want to get into the middle of it. I linked arms with Dean. "Ready for the pasta plate you mentioned?"

"Definitely." Dean led the way as we walked over to the table.

"Was it just me or was he flirting with you?"

"Really? I didn't think so. And he's married."

"That doesn't stop some people."

"Dean, he was just being friendly."

"Just be on your guard," Dean replied.

"A, I'm always on my guard, and B, you have nothing to worry about. My eyes are only for you." I also wanted to add that Hudson Wiley was very well respected, but I knew that people could show a different side when no longer on public display.

"Just throwing the warning out there. I trust you, I just don't trust everyone else."

"Or anyone else," I added. "Always detecting things."

"Just like a sommelier with wine." A small smile appeared on Dean's face. He turned to the table and picked up two of the pasta plates. "Well, wine and pasta." He handed me the appetizer plate that had a small nest of noodles covered in Alfredo sauce and peas. "To my favorite self-described carb-o-holic."

"Ha! Thanks." I had used the term on several occasions, but it made me smile to have Dean use it, too.

"Since you're my personal sommelier, what would you like to pair with this?"

"Let's go with Chardonnay." I looked up at the signs hanging above each of the tables. "How about Bartlett? We have their wines on the list at Trentino."

"My family has a friend there."

"At Bartlett? How have we not talked about this before?"

Dean shrugged, almost a sheepish look on his face. "I don't know, it hasn't come up."

I felt bad for asking the question, but I said it before I thought about it. There was still so much to learn about each other, but that's why this weekend was key. There would be time to chat without the stress of work or studying. Well, at least not too much studying.

Dean held his glass toward the pourer but then pulled it back. "Wait, are we attending a wine seminar after this? Hudson mentioned one."

"Of course. I want to attend every seminar offered this weekend." Not only was it a way to learn facts that I might not know, it was the opportunity to taste wines from vineyards all over the world. "Each one will usually have three to six glasses from different wineries."

"That's a lot of wine for me today. Maybe I should slow down and skip the Chardonnay."

I glanced at Dean's glass. "You've only had a one-ounce pour. Take as little as you want, but be sure to try everything. There's nothing wrong with tasting and spitting out the wine. Moderation is key." It felt strange to be lecturing a member of law enforcement on drinking, but I wanted to make sure Dean didn't feel like he had to keep up.

"Will it be an issue if I spit out the wine?"

"No, not at all. A lot of the wineries expect it, especially at a festival. That way you don't get intoxicated and you can taste of lot of wines. Listen, there's a lot of great wine here this weekend and I don't want you to miss out. It's going to be a wine-filled weekend,

44

but we'll both drink in moderation."

"There's one catch," Dean said slowly. "You mentioned you wanted to go to every seminar, but unfortunately we'll have to miss some on Saturday for the surprise. I'm sorry I didn't ask you before."

"No, that's okay. I'm excited to see what you have planned. Do I get a hint yet?"

"Not yet, but I promise you'll be happy. I want to make sure the weekend goes well."

"It will." I turned around and noticed that the lady in the white dress was no longer tracking Hudson's every move. Her entire focus was on me.

THREE:
PAIRING SUGGESTION:
ZINFANDEL —
LODI, CALIFORNIA

Prior to Prohibition, Zinfandel was the
most planted varietal in the state.

After the opening ceremonies, we headed
inside the New Sierra Hotel for the wine
seminars.

"The History of Zinfandel or Syrah versus
Shiraz," said Dean, as he read out the list-
ings. "What's the difference between Syrah
and Shiraz?"

"Shiraz is what they call Syrah in Australia."

"Ah, noted," said Dean. "Do you have a
seminar preference?"

"Zin, for sure." Not only was it the one
hosted by Hudson, but I also had an affin-
ity for Zinfandel, the red grape grown in
California with a jammy quality to it.

"The Whittier Ballroom, II."

The hotel's larger ballrooms were divided
into smaller rooms by floor-to-ceiling parti-

tions. Rows of tables filled the room and the stage at the front had a long table and six chairs behind it. People slowly filtered in, selecting their seats at the tables.

"There's spots available in the front row," said Dean.

"No way," I replied. "Not in school and not now."

"So you were that kind of student, huh?"

"I was an okay student, just not one who wanted a lot of attention, such as being in the front." I pointed to the third row on the left. "How about there? That way we're close enough but not too close."

"I'm learning more and more about you," replied Dean as we walked toward the third row.

"You were a front-row student, weren't you?"

"No comment." Dean smiled.

Of the four seats, I took the second chair in and Dean took the aisle on my right. Every space had a white paper placemat with six numbered circles and a glass of red wine on top of each.

"How do we know what the wine is?"

I laughed. "They're all Zin."

He nudged me. "Okay, smart girl. But why aren't any of them . . ." Dean didn't say the next part, but I knew he was going to say pink, referencing the slightly sweet White Zinfandel wine.

"These are Zinfandel, not White Zinfandel. As for the wineries, they usually have a numbered list along the side that says what they are." I looked around the placemat but there was nothing.

"They're passing something out," said Dean. He motioned to a lady putting half-size pieces of paper at each seat.

She reached our row and handed us each a sheet. "Sorry about that, meant to have these out earlier."

"No worries." I studied the list and smiled. Of the six Zinfandels we were about to taste, three of them were Old Vines. Zinfandel vines aged well and California had some that were more than one hundred years old. Every glass of Old Vine Zinfandel was a glass of history.

"Look who's a front-row student," said Dean. I followed his gaze to the woman in white from the opening ceremonies. She sat in the seat directly in front of Hudson's position at the podium.

Hudson was trying to look everywhere except at the woman. He wasn't wearing his game face, the practiced pose to hide any and all emotions, but instead looked disturbed, continually rubbing his forehead with his thumb.

"Well, she's persistent, I'll give her that. But look at him," I whispered. "He's clearly bothered by it. She should take a step back. I mean, not in her seat, but the proverbial kind. Hounding him, or anyone, isn't the way to get what she wants."

"Maybe she likes him and is trying to get his attention," said Dean.

"I don't think that's the right way to do it." I watched as Hudson gave a brief but subtle glare to the woman and then focused on the crowd. "I mean, she has his attention, but I don't think it's the right kind."

"Howdy," said a man with gray hair and medium build as he motioned to the two seats left in our row, closest to the wall. "Are those free?"

"They're all yours."

"Great," he said as he walked past with another man with a similar build but whose gray hair was the opposite. Where his receded in the middle but was strong on the sides, the other man's receded on the sides but was strong in the middle. Almost like they were adjoining puzzle pieces.

"I'm Rick," he said as he sat down to my left. "This is Roll." He tilted his head to the second man.

"Rick Roll," I repeated.

"Yep, as in you've been Rick Rolled. Get it?" His reference to the Rick Astley click-bait fad that went around a few years ago cracked him up and the scent of wine emanated as he laughed. Clearly he'd made several return trips to the wine tables at the opening ceremonies. He put out his hand, a huge grin still on his face. "Actually, my name is Walt. No roll. Just Walt." He pointed to his friend. "This here's my buddy Ben. We left the wives at home this weekend."

"Katie Stillwell." I shook both of their hands. My mother told me to always introduce myself with my full name, even though they had only said their first names.

"Dean." He leaned over and shook also.

"And so it begins," said Walt. "Another year, another weekend of wine."

"I take it you've been here before."

He took a sip of all six glasses before answering. "Nearly every year since it began. We missed the first year in 2002, but we've kept it steady since then. How about you?"

"This is our first time to this one." I motioned to Dean and myself.

"Ah, newbies. You'll drink a lot of wine. Here, I'll teach you something."

I smiled as I waited to hear what he was going to say.

50

"Are ya ready?" Walt pointed to the glass. "This here is a red wine." He broke out in a fit of laughter.

I laughed a little as I thought about the number of flash cards on my phone and the knowledge I had. If only Walt knew. I picked up the first glass and sniffed it. It had the classic indicators of Zinfandel with a jammy raspberry and black cherry.

"How do you like the festival so far?" said Ben as he leaned forward to see me.

I glanced at Dean and then back at the two men. "It's good. I mean, it's barely just started. But so far, it's fun."

"We enjoyed the opening ceremonies," said Dean. "I think you did, too." Clearly I wasn't the only one who could tell that Walt had imbibed more than a little.

"Yeah, they run a good show here. I would say this one's our favorite out of all the festivals," said Ben. "We come every year, get the full pass, and spend the weekend drinking wine and smoking cigars in the hot tub at night. Leave all of the stress back in the city."

"Sounds nice," I added, though I wasn't into smoking cigars. I liked the idea of attending a wine and food festival every year, away from stress and without financial worries.

"You smoke the cigars in the hot tub here?" asked Dean in a serious tone. California had strict no-smoking laws regarding hotels and I assumed he was thinking of those.

"No, Ben has a second home about thirty minutes away," said Walt. "This is our annual guys' trip." He slammed his hand down on the table, the glasses of wine clinking together. "Okay, which is your favorite festival?" he said with a smile. "We've told you ours, now you tell us yours."

"Napa," said Dean without missing a beat. I wasn't sure if he had actually attended a wine and food festival before, but I appreciated his quick response.

"Welcome, welcome," said Hudson from the stage. "Let's get started, shall we?" He held his staple red wine in his hand and I had a feeling I wouldn't see him empty-handed the entire weekend. "There might be a few stragglers, but it looks like everyone is ready and since we have all of this fantastic wine in front of us, I say we get started." He turned to the four men and one woman on the stage next to him. "Our panel today consists of the people who made this wine. That's right, the winemakers. So if you have any questions, they should be able to answer them. And if not, we'll throw them out. Or make them pick up our bar tabs." He grinned.

"You'll be leading these one day," whispered Dean. "Master Sommelier Katie Stillwell."

"I have to admit, I really like the sound of that." But as Hudson continued with the panel, the thought of staring out at all those people slightly unnerved me. I had never been on a panel before. But then again, maybe it would be a way to tell the wine's story to a large group. I did love sharing the journey of the wine from the grapes in the vineyard to finally ending up in a bottle to start a new story with whoever opened it.

"Let's start with the first wine. From what I've been told, it's a great one," said Hudson.

I picked up the first glass of Zinfandel, but a commotion near the stage took my attention.

"Sorry. I'm so sorry," said the woman in the front row as she stood up, her focus finally no longer on Hudson. Her white dress had a large patch of red wine down one side and the two people next to her were trying to dab marks from their clothing. "I'm so sorry," she repeated.

"We need cleanup," said the man with horn-rimmed glasses who was on stage with

Hudson at the opening ceremonies. He walked down the aisle, a radio to his lips.

"Don't worry, we'll get it all taken care of and pour everyone new glasses," said Hudson into the microphone. "Not everyone can hold their liquor as well as others." He laughed, but the statement didn't come across as friendly.

The two seated ladies near her looked annoyed, their clothing clearly stained.

"Excuse me." The woman in white moved out of her row and briskly walked down the aisle toward the exit, her expression on the verge of tears.

"Poor girl," I said to Dean. "It's an easy thing to do, to tip over the glasses. You move your hand wrong and all of them can go down."

He nodded. "Just you be careful."

I motioned to the glasses in front of him. "You too, Detective."

"As soon as we get more wine in the front, let's talk about some Zin, shall we?" said Hudson, but he wasn't looking at the row. He was staring at the back of the room, watching the woman leave.

FOUR:
PAIRING SUGGESTION:
SAUVIGNON BLANC —
NAPA VALLEY, CALIFORNIA

Grown in a warmer climate, this
wine tends to have medium acidity
and notes of peach.

When the panel ended, Dean and I stayed in our seats as the ballroom cleared. I didn't want to spend several minutes slowly moving with the crowd, so I figured it was best to wait. I took one last sip of the Zinfandel from Paso Robles. It was more floral than the other five, which came from various regions of California, and it seemed to suit my palate at that moment. The opportunity to taste the exact same grape grown in different areas, therefore each creating a unique wine, was one of the key elements I loved about wine and food festivals.

"Hey, that was fun, being seat neighbors," said Walt. "We hope to see you at the next one."

"Us, too," I replied with a smile.

He hit the table with his palm and pointed. "You can count on it." He shuffled past the chairs.

"I have Zin on the brain now," said Ben as he walked with him. "Zin brain."

When the path was clear enough, we stood up. Hudson was already in the back of the room, drinking the remaining glasses of one particular wine at each seat that was empty during the seminar.

Dean and I walked toward the exit but paused when we reached Hudson.

"Is that a favorite one then?" I said, not able to resist asking.

"The best," he replied. "They'll just pour them out anyway and it would be a shame to let it go to waste." Hudson moved to the next seat and picked up another glass. Along with his excellent memory, he clearly had a very high tolerance.

We moved into the hallway where attendees milled about.

"I'd like to know his blood alcohol level," said Dean.

"It doesn't even seem to affect him. He's like a tank."

"I hope he's not driving," added Dean.

"I'm pretty sure he'll be at the festival the whole weekend. There's no reason for him to leave."

Dean picked up a crumpled piece of paper from the floor. "The list from the seminar."

"I guess someone didn't like the wine."

"Or just likes to litter," replied Dean. "Let me throw this away. I'll be right back."

"I'll figure out where we go next." I took out the schedule, but the seminar was the last event for the day, with activities resuming at ten o'clock the next morning.

I stepped back to look for Dean and my shoulder bumped into someone. "I'm so sorry," I said as I turned around. It was the woman who knocked over the glasses in the seminar. She had changed out of her wine-stained white dress into a black cocktail one.

"It's okay." She smiled, but her dark brown eyes didn't share the emotion. She pulled her hair back and took a deep breath. "Today has not been my day." She seemed different from when she lingered around Hudson at the opening ceremonies. Like the mishap at the panel had broken her in some way.

"Are you doing okay? Don't worry about the wine thing, it's really nothing. Honest."

"Oh." Her smile faded. "You saw that. It was so embarrassing. I don't even know what happened. I turned in my seat to look around the room and suddenly all of my glasses were tipped over." She met my gaze.

"It was terrible."

"Don't worry, they had it cleaned up within minutes and the seminar went on as usual. I bet no one even remembers."

"I remember. Nothing is going like I planned." She looked down at her outfit. "I feel so overdressed right now."

"Everyone is in a whole range of clothing." I motioned to the crowd in the hallway. "Jeans to dresses. You fit in fine."

"At least this dress is black. No one will be able to tell if I knock over more wine."

"Look at it this way, you got it out of the way. Now you can enjoy the rest of the weekend knowing that your spill is already done. We all have to spill at some point."

"Thank you. You're sweet." She put out her hand. "I'm Jocelyn. Jocelyn Rivers."

"Katie Stillwell."

"Katie, it's great to meet you. You've already cheered up my day." She smiled, and it seemed genuine this time. "Now if I can just talk to someone and get a little something cleared up, my weekend will be even better."

I figured she was talking about Hudson, but I didn't want to intrude. "It's only Thursday. I'm sure there will be other opportunities throughout the weekend."

She nodded softly. "I hope you're right. I

really need you to be right."

"What did I miss?" asked Dean as he joined us.

"This is Jocelyn Rivers."

"From the Zinfandel panel," added Dean as he shook her hand.

"Oh great, see, people do remember."

Dean glanced at me with a concerned look on his face, like he had said something wrong.

"Just Dean here. He has a great memory like that. But honestly, you're fine. I'm sorry you missed the seminar, but there will be other ones tomorrow. They're fun and you learn a lot during them."

"Thanks." She sighed. "I guess I just need to shake it off, right? I'm glad I met you. Perhaps I'll see you later?"

"If not tonight, then definitely the rest of this weekend." I paused. "Were you able to get a room at the Lancaster?"

She put her hand to her head. "Oh, you saw that too? You seem to be catching all of my mishaps today."

"We were checking in at the same time."

She nodded but looked embarrassed. "They were supposed to have a room for me, but they didn't. As I said, everything has turned into a mess. I was able to get one here, though."

"Good, I'm glad," I added. I must have misjudged her scene at the front desk earlier. Everyone has bad moments.

"Thanks again," she said. "I'll see you both soon." Jocelyn gave a small wave and walked away.

"I really hope her weekend gets better," I said to Dean. "She was devastated at the whole spilling thing."

Dean nodded. "I think anyone would be. You would be."

"True," I replied.

He smiled. "What's next on the schedule?"

"There aren't any events until ten o'clock in the morning. I mean, not for us. They do some special winemaker dinners you can pay extra to attend, but we're not going to those."

"Are you hungry?" asked Dean. "Downtown Santa Barbara is only forty-five minutes away. We could have dinner there since we won't get a chance to see the city the rest of the weekend."

I thought about the Spanish-style buildings, the red tiles with the white stucco below, as the ocean shimmered in the distance. "That would be great." I paused as I remembered our earlier conversation. "Wait, is this part of your surprise?"

"No, that's planned for Saturday afternoon."

"Can I have a hint?"

Dean held the door open and we walked across the lawn. "Not yet. I want it to stay a surprise."

"I'm looking forward to it."

"Great." Dean brought his hands together in a single clap.

"Oh!" said a lady in a black-and-white pantsuit and long cascading brown curls pulled halfway on top of her head by a clip. "You scared me there."

"Sorry." But as Dean said it, I could tell her exclamation shocked *him.* It had sent a burst of nerves up my arms, too.

"I thought I was out here alone. I didn't expect to see people near me. It gave me quite a fright." She was in her late forties with a nearly chiseled face, as if she didn't smile a lot, and brown eyes that darted around nervously.

"I'm sure people will be going back and forth between the two hotels all weekend. Are you okay?"

"Fine. It will all be fine." She shook her head, her curls moving around. "I just need to watch where I'm walking. I don't even know why I'm out here." She put her hand to her lips and started biting her nails, glancing around as she headed toward the New Sierra.

The back of her outfit had a red wine stain across the white section. She must have been one of the people sitting next to Jocelyn at the Zin panel. Her movements were rapid and full of energy, and part of me wondered if she accidentally knocked over the glasses instead of Jocelyn. It was like blind tasting a wine when you had recently used a fragrant soap on your hands. It hid the aroma of the wine and you only smelled the soap.

Five:
Pairing Suggestion:
Crémant De Limoux —
Languedoc, France

This sparkling wine comes with a lot
of history, as records show it's been
made since the 1500s.

Dean and I had a nice dinner in downtown
Santa Barbara and I even studied my flash
cards in the car on the way back. The
weekend was off to a great start.

When we returned to the Lancaster, I
thought about Hudson's comment of meeting for drinks later. My hopes weren't up
for joining him, but at least sitting in the
bar would be a nice way to round off the
evening. "Do you want to get a drink? It's
still pretty early."

"I'm following your lead."

We headed into the bar, the pale yellow
glow behind the liquor cabinets contrasting
with the dark mahogany wood that lined
the room. People were scattered around but
there were still empty tables.

"How about here?" I motioned to a small table with two round leather chairs.

"What about joining Hudson's group?" Dean nodded toward the cluster of chairs near the fireplace. Hudson sat with a glass of wine in his hand next to Walt, Ben, and three empty chairs.

"I didn't think you were a fan."

"Well, it would help your career to spend time with a Master Sommelier, correct?"

"I guess." Though I knew it would. Not from a network standpoint, but from speaking with him and learning. Every bit of information would help. "Even though he mentioned it earlier, I would feel weird going over there. Like I was imposing. I'm happy to sit here with just the two of us."

"I like that. The two of us." Dean took a seat. "Actually, you have another friend here."

I followed his gaze to Jocelyn walking across the lobby. "That's strange. She said she had a room at the New Sierra."

"It's a festival. I'm sure people wander all over."

"But there weren't any events here."

Jocelyn halted and stood awkwardly at the edge of the lobby near the elevator.

"She probably wants to talk to Hudson. She'll find him in the bar soon enough." I looked over at Hudson. His wineglass was nearly empty and he motioned for the waiter. He met my eyes and pointed to the empty chairs near him. "He's waving us over."

"Told you so," whispered Dean.

"Shut it," I replied with a smile. "Mind if we join him?"

"You know I don't."

We walked over to the group.

"This is Katie and John," said Hudson as we sat down, proving that his memory was not just a rumor.

"Actually, I go by Dean."

"Dean," said Hudson. "Meet Walt and Ben."

"We've met, actually." I smiled at the two of them. "Rick Roll."

Walt cackled at the reference and slapped his knee.

"So he did that to you, too, huh?" said Hudson.

"Yep. At the Zin panel."

"You know what I love about Zin," said Ben as he sat forward and made sure that he had everyone's attention. "That sometimes it's peppery and sometimes it's jammy, and" — he paused as he looked at each of us — "sometimes it's both." He sat back in his chair and nodded as if clearly pleased with his comment.

"Thank you for that, Ben," said Hudson. "Another brilliant deduction."

"Is this seat available?" said a voice next to me. It was Jocelyn.

I glanced at Hudson, not sure what to say. I knew there was some tension between them and I didn't want to overstep my bounds by inviting her to sit down.

"It is," said Hudson, his game face clearly on. "Join us."

"Thank you." She sat down and smiled politely as she put her large bag on the floor. "Jocelyn," she said to Walt and Ben. I expected them to reply with their Rick Roll joke, but they both just nodded.

Hudson stood up from his seat. "I'll be back. I have to make a call."

Dean motioned to the glass in Walt's hand. "Is this one of the same wines from the seminar? A Zin?"

"No, it's a Syrah," replied Walt. "But how about those Zins today?"

As their conversation continued, Jocelyn sighed and turned to me. "I don't think he likes me."

"Dean? No, I think he's fine. He's trying to learn more about wine." I looked at Dean. He was embroiled in the conversation with Walt about the seminar while Ben

66

was about to fall asleep.

"No, not Dean. Hudson. I think it's that I come on too strong. I don't mean to, I just thought that was the way to get him to talk to me." She shook her head. "But at least now we're chatting. I mean, if he ever comes back." She smiled at me. "As you said earlier, we have all weekend."

I glanced at the festival pass still hanging from her neck. It had a gold bar around the edges, noting that she had purchased the highest level with early entrance to the tastings. "We do. Besides the earlier mishap, are you enjoying the festival?"

"Sure." She picked up the pass and looked at it. "I put nearly every penny I had into getting this. I thought it would be a fun weekend away, but it hasn't been fun yet. But there's still time." She looked over at Dean. "You guys make a cute couple. How long have you been together?"

"Not too long." I leaned closer to her. "Actually, it's our first weekend away."

"I love that you chose a wine and food festival. Is it going okay?" Her eyes were soft and she looked concerned.

"Why, does it look like it's not?" I glanced at Dean. He seemed happy, talking to Walt.

"No, it's great. I just find that things out of routine can be awkward, know what I mean? I see a lot of people like that where I work. It's their first time doing something together and they're not sure how to act, that's all." She took a deep breath. "I'd love to have a boyfriend here with me. Or a man-friend." She smiled at her joke, but her attention was distracted as Hudson returned to the group.

"What did I miss?" he said as he sat down. "Any more moments of genius from Ben?"

Ben put his hand up like he was about to say something. "No. Still thinking."

"Good, you keep thinking then. In fact, there aren't enough drinks here. You want wine?" He motioned to me and Dean, and the gesture seemed to include Jocelyn, but I wasn't sure.

Hudson waved to the waiter, who approached and stood to Hudson's side. "Ready for another round?"

"We are," said Hudson. "Let's do another one of these." He motioned to his glass. "The Rioja." He turned to Jocelyn. "What would you like?"

Jocelyn's face lit up. "Um, something red?"

"Cab okay?" asked Hudson.

"Whatever you suggest."

Hudson looked at the waiter. "She'll have

the Napa Cab. What about you, Katie? Dean?"

"A glass of Pinot Gris," I replied.

"Same," said Dean.

"Great," replied Hudson. "New buddies, Rick and Roll? Any drinks for you?"

"This is the last one," said Walt as he motioned to the half-empty glass of wine in front of him. "Then we're gonna Rick Roll right outta here."

Ben pointed to his glass, but it was already empty and it puzzled him for a moment but then he shifted his focus to his pointing hand.

"That's right, you're not staying here." Hudson looked back at the waiter. "That'll be all."

"I'll be right back with those," said the waiter.

Jocelyn leaned over to me. "You were right. It's getting better already," she said in a relaxed tone.

"Actually," said Walt as he downed the rest of his wine and put some cash on the table. "We'll go now. I hear a couple of cigars calling our name." He put his hand to the side of his mouth. "Walt . . . Ben . . . Can you hear them?"

"I can hear them," said Ben as he sat up.

"Are you driving?" asked Dean, his professional instincts kicking in.

"Cabbing it the whole weekend," replied Walt.

"Good, I'm glad," added Dean. "See you gentlemen tomorrow."

"You most definitely will." Walt saluted and Ben did a smaller wave.

"Drink lots of water tonight," I said as they walked away. "Maybe a B vitamin, too." But they were already out of earshot.

"Why a B vitamin?" asked Jocelyn.

"I find that it helps keep away hangovers."

"Ooh, I'll have to try that," she replied, as her eyes grew wide with excitement.

"Two down, but those seats won't be empty for long," said Hudson. "This is a festival after all. But hey, we have the four of us and wine is on the way."

The waiter arrived with the drinks and placed them on the table in front of each of us. Hudson picked up his glass of Rioja and lifted it toward us. "Cheers. Here's to the festival."

"To four days of fun," I added.

"To new friends," said Jocelyn.

Dean glanced at the three of us, a level of uncertainty on his face as he thought about what to say. "To learning more about wine."

We all clinked glasses and I took a sip of my Pinot Gris. It had flavors of apple and lemon but high heat, which clued me in that it was from California. "Is this from Santa Barbara?"

"Santa Rita Hills," replied Hudson, citing the nearby wine region.

Jocelyn's drink was still in her hand, untouched, as she waved at a lady who passed the bar area. She noticed me watching. "Just an old friend," she added.

"I didn't know you had friends here," I replied, not meaning to say it out loud. She had seemed so alone and almost lonely before. "We have empty chairs. Have her join us," I added, in an effort to recover from the statement.

Jocelyn shook her head. "It's not like that. But if you'll give me just a moment." She picked up her bag and left the bar.

Hudson leaned back in his chair as soon as she was gone. He took another drink of his glass of Rioja. "Who's up for some blind tasting?" he said. "Dean, want to give it a go?"

"No, thank you. I'll stick with this Pinot Gris." Dean had barely tasted it. I had never seen him drunk or even tipsy and I had a feeling I never would. In fact, it was almost weird to see him drink. He was similar to my father in a lot of ways, but my father

71

sometimes had a glass of Scotch after a hard day.

Hudson looked at me. "Katie, what do you say? A blind tasting in anticipation for Tuesday?"

I glanced at my glass of wine. "Although it would be great, I don't know. I don't feel like I'm in the right mindset, and I have this Pinot Gris here that I've barely touched." Being at the festival with Dean, I had taken it very easy on the drinking. I wanted to make sure everything went well and although I had a high tolerance, it wasn't worth risking it.

"The Pinot Gris can wait," said Hudson. "A Master Sommelier offers you a chance to blind taste with him and you're going to turn him down? You're a different one, Katie Stillwell."

I sat up straighter in my chair. "I like being different." I put the glass on the table. "And I didn't say I wouldn't. I just said I wasn't in the right mindset. But let's do this."

Six:
Pairing Suggestion:
Gewürztraminer —
Monterey, California

A popular wine for blind tasting due to
its intense aromas such as lychee.

Hudson waved over the waiter and pulled
him close, whispering his wine orders.

"I get to see your blind tasting skills in action. This will be a treat," said Dean. He
knew about my blind tasting group, but I
had never gone through the process with
him. "Nervous?"

"No," I lied, but even I could hear the
tremor in my voice. I had never blind tasted
in a one-on-one session with a Master Sommelier before. It would be unnerving to say
the least, but the test was only days away
and it would be good practice. "Okay,
maybe a little."

"You'll do great," whispered Dean. "I
know it."

Jocelyn returned to the table. "What did I
miss?"

"Hudson's ordered wine and Katie's going to tell him what it is."

"Wait, how?"

I was about to respond, but I could tell Dean wanted to so I waited.

"She's going to taste and tell him the location." He looked at me as if he was making sure he was right. "The type of wine, I mean the grape, and the year."

I nodded. Dean had paid attention when I told him about the blind tasting process.

Jocelyn stared at me with admiration. "You go, girl. I want to see this."

I smiled, but I could already feel my lungs begin to tighten. I hoped the Masters wouldn't be sitting this close on Tuesday.

The waiter arrived with two glasses, one red and one white, and placed them on the table in front of me. I moved my Pinot Gris in front of Dean and stared at the two glasses.

"Are you ready?" said Hudson. "Don't freak out, but I'm already judging you."

"Seriously?"

Hudson laughed. "Doesn't matter. Ready?"

I nodded. "Bring it."

He clicked the timer on his phone and I picked up the first glass, tuning out everything around me.

"This is a clear white wine with a pale gold color and high concentration. There are no flaws on this wine."

I held the glass to my nose and took a deep breath, taking in all the aromas. "On the nose, apricot, peach, tangerine, honeysuckle, potpourri, and" — I paused as I discerned the spice — "gingerbread."

"On the palate." I took a long sip and swished the wine around, the flavors intensifying as I did so. "On the palate, confirm the apricot, peach, tangerine, honeysuckle, potpourri, and gingerbread. Minimal acidity, full body, high alcohol, complexity medium plus." I was already pretty sure it was a Viognier from California, but I needed to complete the process. Viognier was also grown in Condrieu in France, but it had a stone and granite quality. This one didn't and had higher alcohol, which was characteristic of California wine.

"Initial conclusion, this is a new world wine, one to three years." I stared at the glass in my hand and swirled it, the golden liquid climbing the sides. "Possible varietals include a Chardonnay from California, a Viognier from California, and a Pinot Gris from Oregon." Although I had options on where I could go with this, I felt confident it was a Viognier.

"Final conclusion, this a 2016 Viognier from California, the Carneros area, quality level good." I put the glass of white wine down and picked up the second glass. "This is a red wine with . . ." I continued through the process, my entire focus on the contents of the glass and not the audience around me.

"Final conclusion, this is a 2015 Beaujolais from Morgon, France, quality level good." I put the glass on the table and looked up at Hudson, my heart pounding. I noticed Dean and Jocelyn looking at me out of the corner of my eye, but I kept my focus on Hudson.

He stopped the timer and stared at me. "You really are a different one, Katie Stillwell."

"I'm going to continue to take that as a compliment. How did I do?"

"How do you think you did?"

I glanced at the glasses. I felt confident during the tasting, but it could have been a false confidence, brought on by the decision to tackle the wines without doubting myself. The first wine came across as a California Viognier and the Beaujolais had granite and cherries. I needed to trust my call. "I think I did well, but there's always room for improvement."

Hudson motioned to the two wines. "You passed with flying colors. One is a 2016 Viognier from California and the other is a Beaujolais from Morgon." He nodded at me. "I look forward to seeing you at the exam. Though, if you knock it out of the park with the six glasses like you just did with these two here, it will be a cake walk for you."

"Thanks." I smiled as my confidence about Tuesday increased. I moved the two glasses to the side and returned to my Pinot Gris. My hand was shaking. At least it was steady when I went through the blind tasting routine. Maybe that's how the test would be. By focusing and pushing away my anxiety, I was able to concentrate on the task at hand, but the anxiety was still waiting, so it came in once I was done. I could be okay with that.

"The Palate," Dean whispered in my ear, noting my nickname given to me by my blind tasting group.

"That was neat," said Jocelyn. "I never could do something like that."

"You could," I replied, my heart still racing, though I could feel it slowing. "It's training yourself to do it. You learn the different characteristics of each wine, and then the scents of fruits, flowers, and such, and then you look for them in the glass."

"Exactly," said Hudson. "In fact, we have a blind tasting seminar on Saturday. You should attend," he said to Jocelyn.

She sat up straighter. "Are you hosting it?"

Hudson's attention was across the lobby. "Speaking of the festival, here comes Mr. Tinsley."

The man I saw earlier on stage with Hudson approached the table. "Mr. Wiley."

"Mr. Tinsley," Hudson responded. "Won't you join us?"

"Thank you for the offer," he said as he adjusted his round horn-rimmed glasses. "But I don't have time." He enunciated every word as he spoke, as if he had a slight British accent or had taken polishing lessons. "My full attention is needed at every turn this weekend."

"Surely you can join us for a drink. The seminars are done for the day and even all of the wine dinners must have finished by now."

Mr. Tinsley looked around, adjusted his glasses again, and took a seat. "I'll stay for a few moments and then I must go."

"I'm glad," said Hudson. "Let me introduce you around. This is Dean and Katie Stillwell."

"Nice to meet you both," said Mr. Tinsley as he shook our hands. "You're pouring for us on Sunday, correct? And Dean Stillwell, I believe you're volunteering?"

I suppressed a laugh at the mention of Dean having my name. "Correct on both counts," I replied.

"And this is . . ." Hudson hesitated as he motioned to Jocelyn.

"Jocelyn Rivers," she said.

"It's lovely to meet all of you. I trust you're enjoying yourselves at the festival?"

"Having a great time," said Dean.

"Me, too," added Jocelyn, and she looked like she meant it. The earlier spill was in the past and I was glad. I took a sip of my Pinot Gris and relaxed into my chair, the blind tasting now successfully behind me.

"What can I get you to drink, Mr. Tinsley?"

"Nothing, I'm not staying."

"Come on, Tinsley, the more you drink, the better the festival gets." Hudson glanced at him. "Not that the festival isn't great already."

"Uh-huh, sure, Mr. Wiley. Watch it, buddy," said Mr. Tinsley with a slight smirk. The look on Hudson's face showed that Mr. Tinsley didn't normally talk like that. "I'll pass on the drink, thank you," he added.

Hudson nodded to me. "Katie's a fellow sommelier."

"Really? Here in Santa Barbara?" Mr. Tinsley shifted in his seat to face me.

"No, I'm up in the Bay Area. I work at a restaurant called Trentino."

Mr. Tinsley smiled. "Sounds delightful. Always a pleasure to meet another member of the wine community. Do you work in wine as well?" he asked of Dean and Jocelyn.

"I've just embarked on a new opportunity," said Jocelyn. "It's a little complicated so I'm still waiting to see how it works out, but hopefully it does." It was like she didn't want to answer the question, but there was also something charming about her response.

"What about you, Mr. Stillwell? Is wine part of your life?"

Dean gave a nod. "Katie's a part of my life and wine is her world. So yes, it's part of my life, too."

Mr. Tinsley returned his attention to me. "Let's talk about vino, since I have a quick moment and I enjoy meeting sommeliers. Tell me, what's your favorite element about wine?"

I loved questions like these, though this one was unique and not the usual one asking what bottle sparked my fascination with wine. "My favorite element," I repeated. "That would be hard to narrow down to just one, but I love how it brings people together. I love the history of it and how it dates back centuries. I love how there's a story in each and every bottle."

"She's going to do well in life," said Mr. Tinsley to Hudson. "She has the passion."

"Yes, I do," I replied in an effort to stop the passive aside. I wasn't a fan of when people talked about me as if I wasn't right in front of them.

"Yes," said Hudson. "And she's taking the test this week."

"Is that so?" said Mr. Tinsley as he turned his attention back to me. "Would this be the Master Sommelier Exam?"

"Not yet. I'm taking the Advanced Exam on Tuesday."

"I'm proctoring the test," added Hudson.

Mr. Tinsley motioned to Hudson. "Perhaps buy him a drink. Get on his good side this weekend." It was nice that Hudson was now the subject of the asides.

"You know I'm a standup guy, especially when it comes to the exams. I never bend the rules on anything in life."

"I know, Mr. Wiley. It's why I hired you." Mr. Tinsley looked at me. "But getting on someone's good side never hurts. Buy him some wine. Perhaps a nice Syrah."

"I can hear you," said Hudson.

Mr. Tinsley grinned. "I should get going, but it was lovely meeting you, Ms. Stillwell, Mr. Stillwell, Ms. Rivers. I'll leave you to your drinks." He stood up. "If we don't happen to cross paths again this weekend, I do hope you enjoy the rest of the festival."

"I'm certain we will," I replied. "It's clearly very well planned and organized."

"Did you hear that, Mr. Wiley? It's well planned."

"I never said it wasn't, Tinsley," replied Hudson.

Mr. Tinsley smiled and walked away.

"We go back a long time," said Hudson. "He plans a great festival."

Jocelyn leaned toward him. "The blind tasting session you mentioned. Are you hosting it?"

"I am," replied Hudson. "You should attend. There's a lot you can learn."

She smiled. "If I order a glass of wine for you right now, will you be able to tell me what it is?"

Hudson leaned closer. "I might."

I looked at Dean. He seemed uncomfortable by the whole interaction, and he wasn't alone in the feeling. I glanced at my watch. It was late and wine seminars started at ten o'clock in the morning. "This was a lot of fun, but unfortunately we have to go," I said as I stood up.

Dean placed two twenties on the table in front of Hudson. "This should cover it with tip. Thank you for the wine."

"What about these?" asked Jocelyn, as she pointed to the two glasses from the blind tasting. I had only taken small sips so they were nearly full.

"You're welcome to them."

"Perfect." Jocelyn moved the glasses in front of her.

"Night," said Hudson. "Catch you in the a.m." He returned to his conversation with Jocelyn.

"They seem to be getting along now," said Dean.

"True," I replied as we walked through the lobby, past the bellhop. "She was so desperate to talk to him and he wanted nothing to do with her, yet now he's chatting like they're good buddies."

"Maybe he changed his mind," said Dean.

"Or maybe the wine changed it for him." I glanced back at the bar. Hudson and Jocelyn were still talking, closer than before. "Either way, it will be interesting to see how they are tomorrow."

SEVEN:
PAIRING SUGGESTION:
BARBERA D'ALBA —
PIEDMONT, ITALY

This red wine has low tannins with
notes of cherry and strawberry and
is best consumed young.

It was close to nine o'clock in the morning
as Dean stood near the door, already
dressed in a white polo shirt and jeans.

"You look like you're ready for work."

Dean looked down at his outfit. "What's
wrong with jeans and a polo?"

"Nothing. But it does remind me a little
of your uniform. Are you ready to solve
some crimes?"

"I hope not," replied Dean. "I'm on vacation. The only thing on my mind is breakfast."

"Nearly ready. Give me two seconds."
Even though I would probably come back
up to the room after breakfast, I wanted to
make sure I looked ready to face the day.
The dining area would most likely be filled

with guests going to the festival, and Hudson or Mr. Tinsley could be around. It was smart to look my best. I was already in my gray slacks and top, but I finished putting on eyeliner and ran a brush through my hair one more time. "Ready," I said as I stepped into the room.

"You look nice," said Dean. "As always."

"You're sweet. As always."

We walked into the hallway, the floral print wallpaper a nod to the classic charm of the hotel.

"You could redecorate your apartment with this paper," said Dean.

"Shut it."

"Fine, I'll put it in my apartment."

"Seriously?"

Dean smiled. "Why not? I've been thinking of redecorating."

I looped my arm in his as we walked toward the L shape of the hallway where it turned toward the elevator.

"Is it too much to hope that there's something bland for breakfast?" I remarked.

"Bland?" said Dean. "Don't you mean something delicious and filled with flavor?"

"Okay, not exactly bland, but just not greasy. I really hope they have oatmeal. That's what I want."

"You're weird," said Dean as he nudged me.

"Weird is awesome," I replied.

"Okay, I agree," he said. "But come on. You mean you wouldn't eat eggs and bacon if they have it downstairs? What if it's the best eggs and bacon you've ever tasted in your life? You'd be willing to miss that opportunity?"

"But if I don't taste them, I won't know they're the best eggs and bacon ever." I put my hand up. "All I'm saying is if they have oatmeal, that's what I'm going to eat."

"What's the fun in that?"

"What do you mean? Oatmeal is great and healthy for you." I winked at Dean. "Also, a greasy breakfast, such as bacon, will affect your taste buds for the wine. I want to be ready to taste at the ten a.m. seminar. It's all about white wines from Austria, like Grüner Veltliner, and I love those." I glanced at him. "You might like Grüner. It's kind of similar to Sauvignon Blanc."

"I like any wine that you're introducing me to."

"Are you trying to win the best festival partner award? Because I think you're going to get it easily."

We turned the corner and at the far end of the hallway near the carpeted stairs down to the lobby, a woman sat next to one of the doors in a deep sleep, her legs stretched out, her arms by her side, and her head propped back against the wall.

"Looks like someone didn't make it home last night," said Dean.

"Maybe she was too drunk to get to her room and decided to crash here instead," I said.

We passed the elevator and approached her, but as we got closer, I recognized her dark hair, her black cocktail dress, and the gold edges of her festival pass. It was Jocelyn. I quickened my pace, thinking I could help her get into her room, but as we approached, something didn't look right. Perhaps it was the way she was slumped against the doorframe with a bottle of wine in her hand. Or maybe it was the fact that her face was pale, and not just in the way of someone feeling sick.

"Dean." I put my hand on his arm and stopped walking, only a few feet away.

"I know," he said as he moved forward, reaching her and crouching down.

I ran the last few steps and joined him. "Jocelyn? Are you okay?" I touched her shoulder but recoiled as I already knew the answer.

Dean held her wrist. "There's no pulse."

I looked up at him, but his phone was already out and he was dialing 911. "Alcohol poisoning?" I glanced back at Jocelyn and noticed the dark pool of red at the base of the door. "Dean . . ."

He nodded, phone to his ear, his hand on my shoulder, gently pulling me away from the body. He had already seen the blood. "We have an incident here at the Lancaster Hotel."

A couple exited the elevator and turned toward us.

"Stay back," I said as I motioned to them. "You don't want to see this." I had seen a few dead bodies over the past year and I wanted to save other people from the experience. There are things in life that you can't unsee. Moments that flash into your mind when you least expect them, forcing you to relive the incident over and over again.

"Is she okay?" asked the woman as she continued to approach, the man's hand on her back.

"No," I replied.

"Authorities are on the way, but we need to keep this area secure," added Dean as he ushered them back toward the elevator.

A maintenance man walked up the stairs that led one floor down to the lobby.

"Can you let the front desk know that

there's . . ." I paused as I thought what to say. "A problem up here and the police are on the way?"

The man just stood there, staring at Jocelyn.

"Move!" I yelled. "Go tell the front desk. Tell the manager. We have a dead body here on the second floor!" I didn't mean to yell, but the gravity of the situation was sinking in. Jocelyn just wanted to attend the festival and talk to Hudson. Now she was dead.

The maintenance man scurried down the stairs, but the couple remained, watching like a pair of hawks. People had a hard time shaking their fascination. It was the same reason drivers slowed down on the freeway to get a glimpse of an accident. They had an urge to look no matter how bad the scene might be.

"They'll be here in a few minutes," said Dean without emotion. He was in full work mode. He turned to the couple in the hallway and stood between them and Jocelyn to block their view. "I want to remind you that you need to clear this area."

They didn't move. The police would lead them away soon enough, but their morbid obsession was hitting a little too close to home. Jocelyn didn't deserve to have her death on display. I stared at her and she moved her head to the side.

"Wait," I said as Jocelyn shifted to the right. "Dean, what's . . ." My voice fell away as I realized it was the door opening.

"Hold up," I said as the door continued to open. "Stop!" I knew that evidence was being disturbed. Jocelyn slid all the way down, leaving a smear of red on the door. "No!" I looked up to see who had opened the door.

Standing in the dark room was Master Sommelier Hudson Wiley.

EIGHT:
PAIRING SUGGESTION:
GRAUBURGUNDER —
PFALZ, GERMANY

A Pinot Gris wine with peach notes
and a subtle amount of spice.

Hudson looked like he had just woken up, his infamous hair pushed up on one side and matted to his head on the other. His eyes grew wide as he stared at us. "What's going on?"

"You tell us," replied Dean.

Hudson's eyes drifted down to the body on the floor in front of him. "Is she okay?"

"No," I replied. "She's definitely not okay. The police will be here soon." I wished it was the first time I had ever said that, but it was almost starting to become routine after the events of the last year.

Hudson leaned down as he put his hand to his mouth. "What happened?"

"Don't touch anything," said Dean. "In fact, why don't you step over here."

Hudson didn't move, his attention still

focused on Jocelyn.

"Mr. Wiley," Dean repeated in a firm voice. "Come over here."

He looked up at Dean and then me. "But I'd have to step over her."

"I'm sure you can do it." Dean's tone and demeanor was just like when we met at Frontier Winery nearly a year ago.

Hudson followed his directions and joined us in the hallway. "I can't believe this." He returned his focus to the body. "Is that really . . ."

"Jocelyn Rivers," I replied. The comment saddened me.

"Yes, yes, I can see that now." Hudson rubbed his forehead with his thumb as he stared at her. "I just didn't recognize her." He paused. "And she's really . . ."

"Deceased," replied Dean. "What time did you last see Jocelyn?"

Hudson shook his head. "I can't believe she's . . ." He motioned with his hand.

"Mr. Wiley, I need you to focus. What time did you last see Jocelyn Rivers?"

"Time?" Hudson looked around. "I don't even know what time it is now."

"It's nine in the morning," I replied, but neither Dean nor Hudson reacted.

"Let's try again," said Dean. "Do you have any idea what time she left your room?"

"My room?" Hudson shook his head. "She didn't come to my room."

I expected Dean to get frustrated by Hudson's lack of answers, but Dean's calm demeanor remained intact.

I motioned to the open door. "Is this her room then?"

"No," replied Hudson. "It's mine." He looked at us, his eyes growing wider. "But she didn't come here. She didn't come inside."

"Seriously?" I asked. "She wasn't in your room last night?" I wanted to believe Hudson, but the fact that she was outside his door told otherwise.

"No. Of course not."

My eyes flicked to his wedding ring and back to his face. "If you're trying to protect someone or guard your reputation —"

"Honest." Hudson's wide-eyed gaze of shock was replaced by a sense of certainty. "She didn't come in here."

"She was still in the bar with you when we left last night," said Dean.

"And she was pretty eager to talk to you yesterday," I added.

Hudson shook his head. "That's a long story."

"Care to share it?" asked Dean.

"Not really."

"I'm sure the police will want to know." I stared at Hudson. "A woman was found murdered outside your door. Everything is going to be on the table."

Hudson took a long, deep breath. "She wanted to talk to me about a new wine company. She started asking me the minute I met her yesterday, about an hour before the opening ceremonies. Wouldn't drop it. I told her I wasn't interested in being a part of it, but she didn't give up. Then last night in the bar, she was normal again. Nothing about jobs or companies. She was actually cool."

"What about when we left you last night?" I asked. "What did you talk about then?"

"Wine, life, I don't know. Nothing out of the ordinary. We had a few more drinks and just chatted. That was it."

"But you left together?" asked Dean.

"No," said Hudson, a clear level of fear in his eyes. "The last time I saw her was in the bar last night." He rubbed his forehead. "I mean, she may have followed me upstairs. I don't remember. She kept saying she wanted to take me somewhere."

"Your room," I added.

"No, it wasn't here. Somewhere else."

"Where?" asked Dean.

"I don't know. I'd been drinking," replied

Hudson in an exasperated tone. "This looks bad."

"This *is* bad, Mr. Wiley," said Dean.

Hudson looked at the open door, as if he wanted to escape back inside. "All I know is that I entered my room alone and the last time I saw her, she wasn't like this."

As much as I wanted to believe Hudson was innocent, his comments over the last few minutes weren't helping. "What else can you remember?"

Hudson glanced up at me. "I don't know. It's all too much to take in right now."

Dean's face didn't change at all. As far as I knew, he thought Hudson was guilty, and a part of me did, too. But there was something about Hudson's scared expression that made me start to waver.

"Okay," I said, deciding it was time to change my approach. If he was innocent, there would have been some noise when she was killed or propped near his door. "Did you hear anything last night or this morning?"

I noticed Dean shift to look at me, but I kept my focus on Hudson.

"No, I didn't hear anything. I slept like the dead," he said as he continued to rub his forehead. "I do that at these events. All of the talking and the wine, I'm out like a light. I can't remember anything."

"The local authorities will have more questions for you," said Dean. "They're only going to get harder."

"I know, I know," replied Hudson. His gaze fell to the floor as he ran his hands through his hair, but the movement was rigid due to the amount of gel that was still there from the night before. He looked at me. "Wait, I did hear something. There was a noise. It woke me up."

"What was it? Can you describe it?" I asked.

"Someone knocked at my door."

I nodded, waiting for more.

"But that was it." Hudson shrugged. "I didn't get out of bed to check who it was. It woke me up and I decided to ignore it. They went away, so I figured someone had the wrong room." He stared at Jocelyn's lifeless body on the floor. "It must have been her. If I had answered it, maybe she'd still be alive."

The elevator door opened and two uniformed police officers exited.

"Finally," said Dean as he headed to meet them.

"What time was the knock? Could it have been housekeeping?" I asked.

"No." Hudson shook his head. "Not unless they clean rooms in the nighttime. It was still dark outside. I didn't close the blinds last night."

"Try to remember everything you can. They'll want details." I motioned to the officers, certain they were the first of many about to descend on the hotel.

Hudson shifted away from Jocelyn. "I hope they don't want to talk too long. I wish this hadn't happened, I really do, but the first seminar is at ten and I need to be there."

The statement shocked me and I nearly stepped back, but I kept my focus on Hudson. "Someone is dead. The seminar should be the last thing on your mind."

Hudson looked at me. "The festival is my reason for being here this weekend. It's the reason for everyone being here."

I motioned to Jocelyn. "Wasn't that her reason for being here, too? Surely you want to help find who did this."

"I do, it's just this whole thing has me rattled. And why outside my door? Because I talked to her last night?" He shook his head. "I should have stayed at the New Sierra."

"It might have happened there, too," I added.

Dean and the officers walked toward us.

"Think I can get a drink before they talk to me? I need something to calm my nerves."

I realized it was the first time I had seen him without a wineglass. The officers arrived at the open door where Hudson and I stood near the body. "That would be a no."

NINE:
PAIRING SUGGESTION:
VIOGNIER —
CENTRAL COAST, CALIFORNIA

Due to the citrus notes, this white wine
may come across slightly sweet,
but it is actually dry.

After I had answered a few questions on
how I found the body, I stepped outside the
hotel to get some fresh air. It was almost
ten o'clock, the past hour nearly a blur. My
lungs were tight and my hands shook, but
there were no vineyards in sight. The organized rows of vines often calmed me and
helped me breathe again, but there would
be none of that today.

Festival attendees crossed the parking lot
toward the New Sierra, either oblivious to
the police activity at the hotel or ignoring it,
their lanyards swaying around their necks. I
was jealous of their blissful ignorance.

Dean left the hotel and walked toward me
with efficiency and purpose, as if he was at
a crime scene. Which, he actually was. "Are

you okay?"

"Sure, I mean, people are just dying, what's wrong with that." I glanced at Dean. "I'm kidding. The whole thing is terrible." I shook my head.

His stoic face showed signs of weakening. "I don't like that these things happen when you're around."

"Me neither, but I'll be okay." I took four long deep breaths, but they didn't make me feel any better. "These things happen when you're around, too."

"It's part of my job."

I nodded. It was starting to almost become routine to me. "You left the scene? Are they almost done in there?"

Dean glanced back at the hotel. "It's not my jurisdiction, so I'm not involved and I wanted to check on you. They're taking photos, talking to Hudson, and getting ready to move the victim."

"Jocelyn. Her name is Jocelyn."

"I know. I was trying to soften it for you." Dean shifted next to me. "I'm sorry I booked us into this hotel. If I had chosen the other one, the main one, this wouldn't —"

"I still would have heard about it and I still would have known it was Jocelyn." I looked into his blue eyes. "Honestly, I'm fine. I just feel bad for her. She was sweet. And Hudson —"

"Hudson is in a tight spot," Dean interrupted. "It will be interesting to see how the situation evolves."

"What do you think will happen?"

"I'm not sure." Dean focused on two guests as they walked past us. "It's fortunate for the festival that this isn't the main hotel."

I stared at the attendees on the far side of the lawn as they entered the New Sierra. "I wonder if any of them know."

"I doubt it. People are innately curious. If they knew, they would be over here, trying to get a glimpse of what's going on."

"True, but still, I'm surprised they haven't come over, considering there's cop cars out here."

Dean shrugged. "Maybe they just want to get to the lectures."

"Priorities."

"Ms. Stillwell, there you are."

I turned around to see Mr. Tinsley. He looked slightly disheveled, his glasses were cocked to the side, and he was out of breath. "I'm so glad to find you. Mr. Wiley is, well, he's preoccupied at the moment."

I nodded. "We were upstairs when . . . It doesn't matter. But yes, he'll probably be a while."

"Herein lies my problem, Ms. Stillwell. There's a seminar about to start." He looked at his watch. "In fact, it should be starting right now."

I didn't reply, unsure of what Mr. Tinsley was trying to say. Was he making sure we attended? He continued to stare at me, waiting for something, but I wasn't sure what.

"Well," he continued. "What do you think? Can you do it?"

"Do you mean, are we going to the seminar?" I glanced at Dean. After we discovered Jocelyn, the idea of attending festival events had fallen by the wayside.

"No," said Mr. Tinsley. "Can you lead it? Mr. Wiley was supposed to, but he can't right now, and I need someone up there who knows what they're talking about. You're knowledgeable and experienced."

"Oh, I don't know." I shifted my feet and looked around the parking lot. "I'm sure there's more experienced people than me here. I'm not the only sommelier at the festival." Why did I say things like that? I knew I should add a different comment but I stayed silent.

Mr. Tinsley adjusted his glasses. "Mr. Wiley spoke very highly of you and I need a sommelier up there to lead the seminar. I can't have this festival go down the proverbial toilet. Not on my watch." He stared at me. "So what do you think, Ms. Stillwell? Are you up for the job?"

Lead a seminar? This would be something new and out of my comfort zone. I generally didn't like being in front of large groups, but I also didn't want the festival to fall apart. It wasn't Mr. Tinsley's fault that Jocelyn was murdered. "Yes," I replied. "I can do it."

"Great, let's get to it." Mr. Tinsley turned on his heels and walked at a brisk pace across the lawn to the New Sierra.

I glanced at Dean. "I'll see you afterward?"

"Katie, I'm coming with you."

"Even with this?" I motioned to the cop cars.

"I'm on vacation and you're my number-one priority." Dean was actually willing to step away from a police investigation for me. The realization was touching, but I didn't have time to process it. Mr. Tinsley was halfway across the lawn.

"I've never led a seminar before," I whispered to Dean as we tried to catch up. "I don't know how to do this."

"You've attended lots of these, right? Just go for it. You know wine. You know what you're talking about. Besides, they're going to love you."

"What if I start to panic up there?" My lungs were already tight in my chest and my heart rate was accelerating.

"Take a breath and keep going. I've seen you handle yourself in stressful situations. You've confronted killers and called out counterfeiters in large crowds of wine enthusiasts. You can lead a seminar."

I nodded. I just hoped Dean was right.

We entered the hotel, Mr. Tinsley barely holding open the door, and then followed right behind him as he sped into the ballroom. It was already full.

"I'll see you after, good luck. You've got this," said Dean as he stopped at one of the rows to find a seat.

Mr. Tinsley marched up to the stage and I took a deep breath before climbing the three steps to join him. I looked out at the crowd. There were at least two hundred people in the ballroom, all of them ready to learn about wine. And I was the one to teach them. I swallowed hard and put on my game face, the calm demeanor I wore at work to hide my emotions.

"Good morning. Sorry for the delay," said Mr. Tinsley. "It's not how I run this festival and it won't happen again. I know you were expecting to see Mr. Wiley for this seminar, but he was called away on business and hopes to rejoin us later today. In the meantime, we'll get started. Your host for this seminar is sommelier Katie Stillwell."

I raised my hand slightly and gave a small wave.

"Ms. Stillwell comes to us from the Bay Area, where she's a sommelier at Trentino Restaurant. She's also about to become an Advanced Sommelier, this week, in fact."

If I pass, I thought, but my game face remained solid.

"Ms. Stillwell, take it away."

I took a deep breath and stepped forward to the microphone. I realized I had no idea what the wines even were. In my haste to get to the ballroom with Mr. Tinsley, I hadn't looked at the name of the seminar. I originally planned to attend the white wine seminar, before Jocelyn's body was found, but the six glasses of red wine on the table told me this wasn't that one. Like an unknown answer on the Advanced Exam, I needed to figure it out. Two hundred attendees were waiting and watching my every move.

"Good morning," I said as I glanced down at the paper next to the wines. I went down the list. They were all Pinot Noir, a staple of Santa Barbara County. Relief flooded through me. I could do this. I knew Pinot. I felt my confidence returning as I pushed the events of the morning away from my mind, if only for the next hour. "Welcome to the Pinot Noir seminar. We have six great wines here, all local from the area." My voice shook a little so I stood up straighter and pretended I was in the Advanced Exam. "Santa Barbara is an excellent region for Pinot Noir due to the extended growing season and the fog that creeps through the mountain pass. It's a difficult grape to grow, but it thrives here. Pinot Noir also happens to be an ideal wine to pair with almost any food. It's known as a universal pairing wine and can complement both heavy and light dishes."

I glanced up at the audience, but their faces were blank. They weren't entertained; they were watching a scared sommelier trying to lead a seminar. This wasn't what they paid for. My lungs tightened further, but I had to keep going.

"Let's start with the first wine." I picked up the glass, relieved that my hand didn't shake as I held it. "As you can see, Pinot is a lighter red wine. This is because it's a thin-skinned grape." But even as I said it, I knew it wasn't coming across right. I didn't want to go through each glass, tasting the wine. I needed something more.

The overhead lights reflected on the red color of the wine in my hand and it gave me an idea. I would take it back to blind tasting and the visual differences.

"If you hold the glass at an angle with the white tablecloth behind it, you'll find that you can see through the wine. One of the distinct qualities of Pinot is that it is a lighter wine, whereas with a bolder red, such as Syrah, which is also grown here in Santa Barbara, you won't be able to see through it."

I glanced at the crowd. Several attendees held their glasses at an angle. My focus drifted to Dean. He was grinning.

"In fact," I said as my confidence increased, "you might even be able to read through the wine." I held the list up behind the glass. "Yep, you can. Now, if this was a Cabernet or any of the darker reds, this would not be possible. It's one of the visual clues we use with blind tasting to identify a wine. The first thing we look at is the color. But before I get more into that, Santa Barbara is known for producing excellent Pinot Noir, so let's all have a taste of the first one, which comes from the Santa Maria Valley."

I lifted my glass and glanced out at the audience. I didn't recognize many of the faces, but I could see Walt and Ben in the third row, though they were busy looking at their wines. There was a lady with dark hair in the fifth row and for a moment, I thought it was Jocelyn, but I knew it wasn't. If Hudson was guilty, that was one thing, but if he was innocent, the killer might be in the room right now, watching me.

Ten:
Pairing Suggestion:
Mencía — Bierzo, Spain

This aromatic red wine holds up well and is ideal for fans of Pinot Noir.

When the panel was finished, I sat down in the chair on the stage. Slumped into the chair was more like it. I was exhausted. The seminar was only an hour, but it drained me being on-point that whole time. Even at the restaurant, I had momentary breaks, but the seminar was a steady stream of focus and attention.

The crowd funneled out of the ballroom as an attendee approached the stage. "I loved everything you said about the wine."

I leaned forward and met her eyes. "Thank you so much."

"I never realized you could read through Pinot Noir. I've always thought of it as just another red wine."

"That was a good seminar," said a gentleman passing by. "Well done."

Another lady around the same age joined the first one. "You have so much passion for wine. It's contagious."

It was what I hoped for every night as I approached tables, that the guests would become as excited about the bottle of wine as I was.

"Where do you work?" asked the first lady. "I want to come to your restaurant."

"I'm up in San Francisco at a restaurant called Trentino."

"Well, shoot. That's really far from me. I live in San Diego." The lady glanced at her friend. "Road trip!"

"Yes! We're gonna come visit one day. Just wait."

"I look forward to it." I took out a packet of business cards from my pocket. "Here's the name of the restaurant. Just so you don't forget." I handed one to each of them.

"Can't wait!" The lady scrutinized the card. "Now how do you pronounce this word again?"

"It's somm" — I waved my hand around — "all" — I put my hands up in the air — "yay."

"Ah, I like that! Sommelier." The one lady nudged the other lady. "Come on, Judy. Let's go read through some more Pinot."

They walked away and I decided it was

time to get off the stage. I went down the steps and a wave of relaxation fell over me. It was great to be on the floor again.

Dean ambled up, a smile on his face. "You did really well. I was so proud of you. I mean, I am proud of you."

"Thanks. I'm not a fan of being on the stage in front of everyone, but I'm glad it went okay. The audience seemed to like it."

"Excellent job, Ms. Stillwell," said Mr. Tinsley as he approached. "I couldn't watch all of it, as I had to check the other seminar, but from what I saw, you're a natural."

"Thank you." I wanted to add that it didn't feel natural, but I decided to stay silent.

"Truly excellent," repeated Mr. Tinsley as he reviewed the paper in his hand. "The next seminar is at two o'clock. Champagne. May I put you down for that one?"

"But what about Hudson?"

"If Mr. Wiley is here, I'll have him host, but I have no idea what his schedule is at this point. If he's not available, can you fill in?"

"Of course."

"Fantastic," said Mr. Tinsley as he made a few notes. "The train is back on the tracks. All systems go." He nodded at us, again at his paper, and walked away.

"Two seminars in one day," said Dean. "Better get used to this. I see a lot of festivals in your future."

"We'll see." We walked toward the ballroom exit. "I wonder if Mr. Tinsley will tell the crowd at the next one what's going on with Hudson."

"Sometimes people are better not knowing."

"I guess. But if Hudson is gone all weekend, they're going to have to tell the attendees something."

"You'd be surprised," said Dean. " 'Called away on business' can mean a lot of things, and if people are focused on the festival, they might not care. It depends on if they arrest him. Right now I would say they're only gathering evidence, so I would assume he'll be back sometime today unless they charge him. Though he might not be up for hosting wine seminars or enjoying the festival."

"No, I think he's going to jump right back in. Wine is his life." I glanced around at the people milling about in the lobby. "If he comes back," I added. I didn't like to think of a Master Sommelier being charged with murder. Or committing murder. And maybe he hadn't.

Dean's phone beeped and his face

changed as he looked at it.

"Everything okay?"

"Yeah, just some more news on the Harper case. It can wait until Monday." He put his phone away and took the schedule from his pocket. "There are two lunches starting soon on the lawn. One with tickets and one without. Shall we head over?"

I was about to reply but stopped when I saw Hudson Wiley standing near the lobby doors, a blank expression on his face. "Look who's back."

ELEVEN:
PAIRING SUGGESTION:
AGLIANICO — CAMPANIA, ITALY

A full-bodied red wine that is best consumed after aging for a while.

Hudson's hair had been smoothed out by water instead of his usual gel and he still looked disheveled compared to his normal appearance.

"Hudson," I said when we were close enough. "Everything okay?"

He stared at me in a daze until the recognition set in. "They asked me some questions. Unfortunately, I don't think I had the right answers. I don't remember much. They might ask me more later, but for now, I can be here." He looked around. "I'm glad the festival is still going on."

"Katie took over for you at the Pinot seminar," said Dean. "She did an excellent job."

Hudson raised his eyebrows. "Wow, thank you. I really appreciate it. I didn't want that whole mess," he said as he waved his hand toward the Lancaster, "to distract from the festival." He turned back to me. "What did you say at the seminar?"

"I went over how Pinot Noir is a thin-skinned grape —"

"No," Hudson interrupted. "I mean about me. Did you say why I wasn't there?"

"Mr. Tinsley said you were away on business and would be back soon."

"Perfect." He nodded and glanced around. "All is back to normal."

"Normal?" replied Dean.

"Where can I get a drink around here?"

"The bar is to your left, but I'm sure you already know that," said Dean. I could tell by his tone that he wasn't happy with the way Hudson was handling the situation. It was a little puzzling to me, too. He didn't seem to care.

"Actually," said Hudson, "it should be time for the lunch." He took out his phone. "In less than ten minutes. At least I've only missed one activity. Let's go over to the main tent now. I can get you guys in early."

"Perhaps you should take it easy and rest," said Dean.

The question was pointed. I knew first-hand that interrogation was exhausting, yet Hudson seemed to have bounced back like nothing had happened.

"Rest? Why? There's a festival. Come on." He pushed through the lobby doors without a care in the world, as if someone hadn't just been murdered.

I looked at Dean. "Want to follow him?"

"Absolutely."

We left the hotel and headed across the lawn to the lunch tent, where Hudson was already waiting at the entrance near the line of people.

"Hudson, is it true you were questioned by police?" said a lady from the front of the line.

"I heard someone died," said a man nearby.

"Committed suicide, I heard," said another attendee.

"No, it was two people," said someone else.

"Now, now," said Hudson as he put out his hands. "Ladies and gentlemen, let's focus on the wonderful wine and food we're about to enjoy. In fact" — he paused as he stepped inside the tent and returned with a bottle of wine — "this one's on me. Who wants wine?"

The volunteers handed out glasses and people held them forward, waiting for Hudson to pour a splash of wine. One bottle wouldn't go far with this many people.

"You're more experienced at this than me," I whispered to Dean. "But do innocent people act as nonchalant as this?"

"Death can do strange things to people." Dean's focus was on Hudson, and I could tell he was studying every little movement.

"It just doesn't feel right," I added. "It's common decency to show a little respect for the deceased."

"Think back to the Pinot seminar," said Dean. "No one would have been able to tell you found a dead body this morning. You were wearing your game face, as you call it?"

"I guess." I watched Hudson pour wine for the guests with a practiced smile on his face. "You think he's guilty?"

"Verdict is still out," replied Dean.

Hudson emptied the rest of the bottle. "Sorry, folks, that's it for now. But I'm sure they'll open the doors in just a few minutes." He waved us over. "Want to go in?"

"Sure." I turned to Dean. "Ready for the festivities?"

"You mean the questioning?"

"Why do you say that?"

"I know you, Katie Stillwell. I know how you work."

I thought I saw a flash of a smile on his

face, but it was gone before I could fully register it. "Don't pretend like you don't want to ask him more questions, too. I know you, Detective Dean."

"That's Detective Stillwell to you at the moment. Come on."

Hudson opened another bottle as we entered the tent. He held out two glasses.

"Thanks," I said as I took one. "Hey, did you remember where Jocelyn wanted to take you last night?"

"No," said Hudson as he poured the white wine. "This is a local Chardonnay. The winemaker does a great job of highlighting the baked yellow apple in it."

I waited to take a sip. "So nothing on where she wanted you to go?"

"You guys are starting to sound like the police."

I was about to point out that Dean was in law enforcement but decided to keep that gem to myself for now. "Just curious, and we're only trying to help. A murder investigation, or even just being on the suspect list, could be devastating for your career."

"You come across as a man who likes to protect his reputation," added Dean.

Hudson's face changed. "It might look like I don't care, but I do. Although I didn't like the way Jocelyn went around things the past month, trying to get her business going the way she did, I'm sorry that she's gone."

"Wait, the past month? I thought you just met her yesterday?" The realization shook me and even Dean lowered his glass.

"No, I met her a few years ago at a festival up north. I don't remember it very well, but she reminded me of it yesterday at the opening ceremonies. When I met her before, she was thinking about getting involved with a wine company or something. Apparently, I told her to go for it. Sounds like me. I'm always trying to encourage people in their careers in wine. I didn't think she would come after me, insisting I be a part of it."

"What did she do the last month?" asked Dean, his tone flat.

Hudson took a swig of his glass. "She came to my house in Denver a few weeks ago. Actually knocked on my door and my wife answered. Sarah was none too happy about that. It led to a fight later. She started asking me all sorts of questions about my work trips, doubting me. It wasn't good."

I waited to see if Dean had more questions, but he was silent. "You said Jocelyn insisted you be a part of a company. What was it?" I asked.

"Oh, she wanted to have my name all over it for barely any money. I didn't want that. I have a reputation to protect. Her whole business model was based on the idea that she would use my name to push her wine. No thanks. I don't care how much she wanted a business to succeed, she went about it in the wrong way."

The tent doors opened and the crowd flooded in. Hudson put back on his festival smile and held his arms up as he stepped toward the entrance. "Welcome, wine lovers!"

"May I give my expert opinion now?" said Dean as he kept his focus on Hudson.

"Sure."

"I think he's guilty."

"As a detective, aren't you supposed to remain unbiased in these cases until presented with all the facts?"

"It's not my case. And it's not yours, either." Dean's phone beeped with a text. He looked at it and his face shifted into concern.

"Everything okay?"

"Yeah, I have to take a call. I'll be back." He stepped outside while Hudson laughed with the guests as he directed them to the different food booths even though police cars were only two hundred yards away and an attendee was deceased. I looked around the crowd. No one seemed to care, especially Hudson.

His actions were getting to me. It could just be for the festival, to keep it going, but what if he really was guilty? Would he murder again?

Dean entered the tent, an ashen look across his face.

I had seen it before and knew it meant bad news. My heart rate accelerated and lungs tightened. "What happened? Did someone else die?"

"No, nothing like that. I'm sorry, Katie, but I have to go."

Twelve:
Pairing Suggestion:
Chenin Blanc —
Stellenbosch, South Africa

Chenin Blanc, also called Steen, is
South Africa's most planted varietal.

"There's a potential breakthrough related
to the Harper case and I have to go check it
out," said Dean.

I tried my best to swallow my disappointment but it showed through. Our conflict-
ing schedules left little time together and
even though this weekend was supposed to
be different, work was always there. "You're
driving back to San Francisco?"

"Los Angeles."

The statement made my stomach drop.
My father and his wife lived in Los Angeles
and although he was set to retire soon from
law enforcement, he was still active as far as
I knew. "You're not meeting my father, are
you?"

"No, I would tell you if I were." Dean
looked into my eyes. "I'm going to do

everything I can to get back here for your surprise tomorrow. I wanted this weekend . . ." His voice fell away. "I wanted it to be quality time together, away from our routines, but work —"

"It's okay," I replied, interrupting him. "I understand."

Dean raised his eyebrows. "You do?"

"My father had to leave to go to cases, too. It's part of the job." I smiled and even though I was disappointed, I tried to hide it. "Can you at least grab lunch before you go? It's a long drive." I motioned to the sandwich options of roast beef au jus, herbed chicken, and roasted vegetable.

"Yes, but I want to make sure you're okay."

"Totally fine. Besides, I'll have times when my work or studying gets in the way of plans, too."

"You'll get last-minute calls about breaks in a case?"

I shrugged. "You never know. There might be a bottle of wine that needs to be opened."

Dean smiled and picked up a roast beef sandwich, wrapping it in a napkin.

"A glass of wine for the road, too?"

His eyes grew wide.

"I'm kidding. Hopefully everything works out and I'll see you tomorrow. And if not, I understand."

"I'm really going to try." Dean leaned in closer. "Please be safe here."

"It's a wine and food festival."

"You know what I mean," said Dean with a serious look on his face. "The death of Jocelyn Rivers and the way Hudson is acting. Don't get involved in anything."

"Who? Me? I mind my own business." I smiled, but I wasn't sure it came across as sweetly as I wanted it to.

"Two previous cases tell me otherwise."

"Two cases that I solved, by the way."

Dean's phone buzzed again. "I have to go. If all goes well, I'll see you tomorrow. If not, I'll reschedule your surprise for a future date. But hopefully I'm back." He was already in his work mode as he hugged me, and I felt a wave of sadness when he walked out of the tent, his phone at his ear.

I glanced at the tables. Most of them were full, but I wasn't in the mood for chatting. I grabbed a chicken sandwich and sat at an empty table. I figured more people would join me, but so far, I was alone as I ate.

"Katie," said a female voice behind me.

I turned around, expecting to see a familiar face, but it was a lady in her sixties with tousled short blond hair. I was certain I hadn't seen her before.

"That *is* you," she replied. "I have to tell you, I saw your talk on Pinot Noir this morning. You were great!"

I smiled. "Thank you so much."

"No, thank you! You know, I've always loved Pinot, but the way you spoke about it made me love it even more."

Her statement lifted my mood. "That means a lot. It's always my goal to impart a passion for wine." I motioned to the empty chairs. "Do you want to join me?" I glanced down at her festival badge but there was no name on it.

"No, I'm just on my way out. I already ate and have to meet my friends at the hotel."

I looked at her badge again. The word guest was where the name was usually printed. "I thought all the badges had names on them. Yours looks different."

The lady laughed. "Would you believe it? I lost it yesterday within ten minutes of getting here. I swear I'd lose my head if it wasn't attached to my neck. They had to give me a new one, but I'm just going to pretend it's a special one since it's nameless. Hey, are you doing another seminar today? There's one that starts soon, right? Champagne."

"As of right now, no." I didn't want to say that it depended on further police activity with Hudson, but since he was at the lunch, everything seemed fine at the moment.

"That's a shame," she said. "I want to hear you talk more about wine! Well, it was lovely meeting you."

"Jocie, are you coming?" said a lady the same age with two other ladies nearby. "We're gonna be late."

"Wait." I put my hand on her arm. "Your name is Jocie? As in Jocelyn? That's quite a coincidence."

"Oh, is your name Jocie, too?" She looked at my badge. "No, of course not. Silly me. You're Katie. From the seminar."

"Yes." But the name similarity was too striking. It stirred inside me, like the memory of a wine label I was sure I had seen before but couldn't quite recall.

"I gotta go. Don't want to hold up my friends. We're about to get our wine on before the next seminar."

"Enjoy your wine." I put out my hand. Something inside me said I should get her last name. "It's wonderful to meet you, Jocie. Let me fully introduce myself. I'm Katie Stillwell."

She shook my hand. "It's great to meet you, too. I'm Jocie Rivers."

THIRTEEN:
PAIRING SUGGESTION:
VERDEJO — RUEDA, SPAIN

Often compared to Sauvignon Blanc,
this white wine has citrus flavors and
elevated acidity.

I watched the real Jocie Rivers walk away as the interaction left me in a daze. It would be too much of a coincidence to have two people named Jocelyn Rivers in the area. There were only five hundred people at the festival and the name couldn't be that common.

Dean was already gone and I didn't want to disturb him with a text. He would be driving and focused on the Harper case.

I stared at the exit. Did the Jocelyn I met yesterday pick up the lost badge? If so, was that the reason she was killed? And who *was* she?

I stood up, ready to follow Jocie, but I didn't know if that was a good place to start. She would just repeat that she lost her badge. I could go to the New Sierra where Jocelyn — or perhaps not Jocelyn — said she had a room, but the front desk wouldn't be able to look her up if I didn't know her real name. I doubted she had registered under Jocelyn Rivers.

I thought about going to the Lancaster to tell the authorities that their victim might have a different name, but I wouldn't be able to give them any hints as to who she actually was. I'd made a promise to Dean not to get involved, but if I knew her real identity, I could help the police without getting *too* involved. The desire to find out was like the opportunity to taste a glass of expensive and highly prized wine, like a rare vintage that critics would reminisce about for years afterward.

I scanned the tent. Hudson was busy talking to attendees, and the only other people I had seen Jocelyn with were Walt and Ben.

I left the tent and crossed the lawn to the main lunch event. I didn't have to look far. Walt and Ben sat at one of the picnic benches on the far side of the New Sierra.

"Hey, it's Rick Roll," I said when I reached the table.

"It never gets old," said Walt with a laugh. "I love that my own joke can be thrown back at me."

"Where have you been? The other lunch?" asked Ben.

"Yeah, sandwiches of chicken, roast beef, or roasted vegetables. Not bad."

"Tacos," said Ben as he motioned to the empty plates, his hand knocking them to the ground. "Sorry."

I picked up the paper plates and tossed them in the nearby trash can. I motioned to the bench. "Mind if I sit for a bit?"

"Go for it, but the lunch is done," said Walt. "They might still be pouring, though."

"I'm on wine now." Ben held up his half-empty glass.

"Yes, Ben here had a beer with lunch. Who does that at a wine festival?"

"It was tacos, Walt. Tacos. Beer goes with tacos. Besides, the Champagne panel is next so I'm on wine from here on out." Ben smiled. "There's wine at the panels," he added.

"Very deductive of you, Ben."

He smiled proudly and then pointed at me. "Why aren't you drinking?"

"Soon." I didn't know how to ask them if they knew the real identity of Jocelyn Rivers. I wasn't sure I could come right out and say it, so I decided to try a different tactic. "What are you both having?"

"Chardonnay," said Walt.

"Grown on the sun-kissed slopes of California," added Ben.

"Look at you, getting all poetic about wine," said Walt. "This festival is changing you."

"What do you mean, getting all poetic? I'm always poetic."

"True, and sometimes even correct," said Walt.

"This wine *is* from California and these slopes *are* sun-kissed. I am correct."

"You only know that because you already know what the wine is from the label."

"I don't see a label in front of me." Ben motioned to the table, which was empty except for their two wineglasses. "Do you see a label in front of me?"

"You know what I mean. You didn't figure it out."

It sounded like a reference to blind tasting, and I shifted in my seat. "What's this about?" I asked, hoping I was right and could perhaps ease into the blind tasting in the bar with Jocelyn.

"Apparently silver-tongued Walt here can tell me all about a wine without looking at the label, though I think he cheats."

"You're quoting me incorrectly," replied Walt. "I said I can tell a Paso Robles Zin from any other Zin." He pointed his finger at Ben. "Start listening more."

"I will when you start speaking in complete sentences."

"Don't hold your breath."

"Is that where you live? Paso?" I interrupted, hoping to direct the conversation back to wine.

"No. I just love Paso Zin."

I nodded. "I'm a fan as well." It was time to get to the point. "Hey, so remember last night, we were hanging out with Jocelyn Rivers?"

Walt shook his head. "No talking unless you have wine in your hand. In fact, are you even at the festival if you don't have a glass of wine? I don't think so."

"I'm with Walt on this. Not good enough," said Ben as he folded his arms across his chest.

I took a moment to think about how I could make this work. I pointed to his glass. "What's this Chardonnay? Besides being sun-kissed."

Walt looked at it and swirled. "It's a 2015 from Sonoma. A little heavy on the oak, but I dig it."

"Could you tell what it was without looking at the label?" I asked. "The type of wine and the location, not about the oak."

"Well, I knew all about this wine from the

131

person who poured it." Walt laughed. "But I can tell a few, or maybe several wines, without anyone saying what they are, and not just Paso Zin. I'm pretty cool like that."

"You know," I replied, "I can sometimes do that, too."

"Really?" Walt slammed his palm on the table. "Do I hear a challenge?" he said. He cupped his hand around his ear. "Challenge? Is that you? Are you there?"

I suppressed a laugh. "Are you sure you want to do a challenge?" After the blind tasting session with Hudson, my confidence level had increased.

"Why not? It's a wine and food festival. Let's give it a go." Walt looked at Ben. "Get us each a glass of wine, but no cheating. It has to be the same wine."

"Are you buying?" asked Ben.

"The lunch is open bar," said Walt.

"That's right. Then this one's on me." Ben stood up.

"Actually," I said as the blind tasting process with my tasting group went through my mind. Once one of us said the correct answer, it would be over for the other person and they wouldn't get a chance to properly make a deduction. They could only agree or disagree with what was already said. "Why don't you get two different wines, two glasses of each? Are you up for a double tasting, Walt?"

"Twice the fun," replied Walt.

"I can't carry four glasses."

"You can take two trips, Ben. I'd help you but I can't, because then I would know what the wine is and Katie here would accuse me of cheating."

"I most definitely would," I replied.

"Fine. But don't talk about anything while I'm gone. I don't want to miss the fun."

"We'll be waiting." I smiled. When he walked away, I turned to Walt. "Now that wine is on the way, do you know who Jocelyn Rivers is?"

He thought for a second. "Was she the one in the bar with us?"

"Yes. Do you know anything about her?"

"She's at the festival. That's it." He looked around. "Haven't seen her today though."

"She passed away this morning."

His eyebrows went up. "Ah, so that was her. I heard someone talking about that earlier."

"Did you hear anything else or perhaps know more about her?"

"I might." He picked up a bottle cap from the end of the table and rolled it between his thumb and his forefinger on the wood.

"What?"

Walt flipped the bottle cap up and caught it on the back of his hand. "I might know that she talked to someone in the lobby after Ben and I left the bar."

"Who?"

He flipped it again and caught it in the middle of his palm. "Why do you want to know?"

"It's important. I'm . . ." My voice fell away. I didn't want to clue him in too much. "I'm looking into something. Was it a lady you saw?"

Walt tilted his head sideways as he looked at me and flipped the bottle cap again. It landed on the back of his hand without him looking at it. "It might have been."

With every turn of the cap, I not only wanted to win at the blind tasting, I wanted Walt to be a very distant second place. "You're dodging the question," I replied. "It makes you seem suspicious."

"Me? Nah."

"Did you see a man or a woman?"

"A woman. But I'm not saying anything else until wine is here."

I didn't have to stew for long. Ben returned to the table with a glass of white wine in each hand followed by a waiter holding two glasses of red wine.

"I got some help," said Ben as he motioned to the waiter, who put the red wine down in front of each of us. "That's wine A and I'm holding wine B." He held up two white wines. "B is for Ben."

"And warming them up, I see," said Walt as he motioned to the way Ben was holding both glasses by the bowl and not the stem.

"Putting them down, putting them down." Ben placed a glass to my right and then a glass next to Walt and sat down. "Who wants to go first?" He looked at us and closed his hands together like he was patiently waiting. He was our audience, ready for the show.

"Ladies first," said Walt.

"I think I have an unfair advantage," I replied.

He peered over his sunglasses. "Oh, honey, don't start thinking you drink more wine than me. I have the scars on my liver to prove it."

"Okay, fine. I'll go." I thought about what I wanted to find out from Walt. "But let's put some stakes on this. Make it interesting."

"Katie Stillwell, I like the way you think," said Walt.

"If I get the wine right, you tell me who you saw in the lobby and, if possible, point her out."

"The lobby?" said Ben, but Walt motioned for him to be quiet.

"What if you get the wine wrong?"

"If I'm wrong, you don't have to tell me anything," I replied.

He nodded. "Okay, I like this. What about me, if I get the next wine right? What do I get?"

I paused for a moment. "I'm pouring at Sunday's grand tasting. I'll make sure you get large pours instead of the one-ounce tasting we're supposed to do."

"Deal! This festival just gets better and better," Walt said with a laugh. "Okay, let's start the competition."

I picked up the white wine. "Since you like red wine so much, I'll go for the white wine."

"Very classy of you, Stillwell."

I looked at the glass. I might not be studying my flash cards this weekend, but I was getting a lot of experience tasting under pressure. Every glass of wine I blind tasted was a mystery I had to solve. I just hoped Walt would keep up his end of the deal.

FOURTEEN: PAIRING SUGGESTION: BEAUJOLAIS — MOULIN-À-VENT, FRANCE

Beaujolais in this Cru are named after the large historic windmill in the area.

I went through the wine grid, starting with the visual characteristics, then scent, and finally taste. I was glad Ben chose something other than a Chardonnay. It would have been too easy to do the same glass that Walt had been drinking.

"Final conclusion, this is a Grüner Veltliner from Austria, 2016, quality excellent."

I put the glass down and looked at Walt and Ben for the first time since I started the blind tasting. Both of their mouths were slightly open as they stared at me.

"Walt, buddy, you're screwed," said Ben.

Walt sat up and studied his glass of wine. "No, that's fine. I'm still going to do this." He turned to me. "But, girl, you're no amateur at this."

"I've had a little practice. Well, was I

right?" I motioned to the glass.

"Wait," said Walt. "Don't say anything. I want to taste the wine to see if I agree." He took a drink of the wine. "It's acidic and tart. And I totally get the pepper you did. Okay, I agree. Grüner."

I smiled. I wasn't sure if Walt could have called it without me pointing it out first, but I gave him the benefit of the doubt. "Okay, Ben, what's the reveal?"

Ben glanced at us. "Well, you're both right. It's a Grüner Veltliner."

I nodded, my confidence for the exam on Tuesday continually climbing. "Well done, both of us," I said to Walt. I pointed to the red glass of wine. "You're up."

"Do I have to say it like you did? All those fancy steps?"

"Of course not. Do it as you normally do."

"I don't think there's any normal way I do anything, but here we go." He held up the second glass, imitating the way I swirled the wine. He took a long drink, swallowed, and kept smacking his lips together followed by his tongue on the roof of his mouth. "I think this is a red wine."

Ben erupted into chuckles.

"Okay," said Walt. "Shh. I need to concentrate." He took another sip, swishing the wine around so that his lips moved up and down like a rabbit until he swallowed. "I've had this before."

"Yes, you have," said Ben.

"Hey, peanut gallery, pipe down," I replied.

Ben smiled and visually zipped his mouth shut with his hand.

Walt took one more sip. "This is a Syrah. Actually, a Shiraz from Australia." He put the glass down and turned to me. "Let's see what the ringer here has to say."

"Not a ringer. I told you I had an unfair advantage." I tasted the wine as I tried not to let Walt's conclusion sway me. It had flavors of blackberry, plum, and raisin along with a high level of alcohol. "I agree with Walt that it's a Syrah, but I don't think it's from Australia." There was a different quality than I was used to from a Shiraz, yet the alcohol was high enough to be from a hot region. "I think this is from here in Santa Barbara. And I'm going to take it a step further. This is a 2015 vintage." I thought about it again for a moment. It was still a newer wine, yet 2017 was too recent and 2016 just didn't seem right. "Yep. 2015 Syrah from Santa Barbara, quality level good." I looked at Ben. "Okay, tell us."

"It's a Syrah," replied Ben. "From Ballard Canyon here in Santa Barbara. I don't remember the year, sorry. But 2015 sounds about right."

"Where does that leave us on our little bet then?" asked Walt.

"Come on," I replied. "Clearly I won."

"I would say it's a draw," replied Ben.

I looked at both of them. "Seriously?"

"Well, I did know it was a Syrah. I thought it was from Australia so I said Shiraz, but I still got the grape right. You've gotta give me that," said Walt.

"Yes, but still. We had a deal." I didn't want to take away Walt's pride, but I also wanted to know about the lady in the lobby.

"Okay," said Walt with a laugh. "I'll tell you what you want to know and you'll still pour a little heavy for me on Sunday. In the name of wine and friendship."

"Deal." I waited for the answer, but Walt just continued to swirl his glass. I wanted to tap my fingers on the table as the time passed, but I clenched them to keep them quiet.

He finally looked up. "The lady in question."

"Jocelyn Rivers," I interjected.

"No, not that one. The woman in the lobby. She came in just as we were leaving. In fact, Ben here held the door open for her."

"Oh, I remember her. Yep, held the door. I'm quite the gentleman," said Ben. "Even when I've been drinking."

"I would say more so when you've been drinking," replied Walt. "We watched her talk to Jocelyn while we waited for our cab."

Adrenaline surged through me, a tickling sensation down my arms. "How long did they talk?"

"Not sure," said Ben. "Our cab arrived pretty quick."

"Who was she?" I said, nearly on the edge of my seat.

Walt drank the rest of his Grüner and put the empty glass on the table. "I don't know."

The hope drained out of me like wine from a cracked barrel. Nothing to be saved. Time and promise, all gone. "Seriously? We did that whole blind tasting duel and you didn't even have the info for me? Forget the heavy pours on Sunday."

"However," said Walt. "I would know her if I saw her again. She's definitely still here."

"How do you know she's here?"

"She had a festival pass," added Ben. "I'll point her out if I see her again, but who knows." He picked up Walt's Syrah and took a drink. "Why do you want to know?"

"Let's just call it a project," I replied. "In case we're not together the next time you see her, what did she look like?"

Ben pointed to the glass of red wine.

"That's not helpful," I said. "I'm not up for another round of blind tasting." I wasn't into playing games and I wanted to save my palate for the Champagne seminar.

"What my friend Ben here is trying to say is that she had red hair. But I think his reference to the Syrah is not quite accurate. Her hair was more the color of Beaujolais."

"Beaujolais, yes. I like that description more." Ben pointed at Walt. "What he said."

"Thanks," I said, not only appreciating the clue, but also the detail. It was a very poetic way to describe someone, referencing the color of a lighter red wine from France.

"My pleasure." Walt winked. "Are you sure you're not pouring anything today?"

"No, only Sunday."

"Are you hosting any more seminars?" asked Ben.

I had forgotten it was even a possibility. Although I had done well on stage, my mind was on the mysterious redhead, though I wasn't going to say that. Besides, Hudson was back. "No, just attending events the rest of the day. The Champagne one next, which starts soon, in fact." I stood up. "Are you both going?"

"We'll see you there in a few minutes.

Gotta finish my wine." Walt looked for his glass, then stared at Ben. The Syrah was nearly gone.

I hoped Walt wouldn't ask for too much wine on Sunday. I didn't want to get in trouble with the festival, but at least I had a clue.

I entered the New Sierra Hotel as a memory flowed into my mind like the stream of bubbles reaching the top of the Champagne glass. The woman in line at the opening ceremonies had red hair. She might be the same one that Walt and Ben mentioned and I needed to find her.

FIFTEEN:
PAIRING SUGGESTION:
SEKT — MOSEL, GERMANY

A sparkling white wine made in the
traditional method used for Champagne.

Champagne seminars were extremely popular at festivals and the Whittier Ballroom was filling up quickly. I scanned the rows, noticing a few people with red hair, but none that could be described as the color of Beaujolais. And then there she was — the lady from the opening ceremonies with hair that fit Walt's description. She was in the fifth row and even had empty seats nearby.

"Is one of those available?" I asked over the first few people to the red-haired lady.

She looked up without any recognition in her face. "Of course."

I shuffled into the row and sat down next to her. "It's good to see you again."

She tilted her head, her green eyes taking me in. "Have we met?"

"Just once. I'm Katie Stillwell." I put out

my hand.

She shook it as she continued to stare with disbelief. "Anita Walcott. Remind me again how we've met? I may have imbibed a little. I love bubbles." She motioned to the glasses in front of her, all six of them halfway empty.

"In the line yesterday, at the opening ceremonies. It was brief. But I have a question for you —"

"Oh, yes!" she exclaimed in a very loud voice. "You were studying."

I nodded as a pang of guilt shot through me. I hadn't looked at my flashcards since.

"Welcome, everyone, to the Champagne and sparkling wine seminar," said Hudson from the stage. "Now, as you may or may not know, it's only called Champagne if it's from the Champagne region of France. If it's from anywhere else, it's called sparkling wine. Even if it's still in France. So today we have two Champagnes and four sparkling wines ranging from Extra Brut, which has very little sugar, then Dry, which definitely has some sweetness, and up to Demi-sec, which is quite sweet. Ah, I can tell by some of the reactions here that people are looking forward to the sweet ones, but let's not get ahead of ourselves."

Hudson continued talking, but I took the opportunity to question Anita. "Did you hear Jocelyn Rivers passed away?"

"Who?"

"A festival guest. She had dark hair just past her shoulders and was wearing a black cocktail dress last night."

Anita's eyes grew wide. "You're kidding! What happened?"

"Didn't you speak with her in the lobby last night?" I asked, ignoring the question. "I think I saw you guys talk, after she waved at you." The last part of my statement was a risk, but I was willing to take it.

"Oh, I didn't know her. I met her at the opening ceremonies. I thought it was sweet that she waved at me, but other than that, I didn't know her."

The comment was not one I was expecting to hear. "You didn't?"

"Sorry, I just met her yesterday." Anita put her hand to her chest. "But wait, she died?"

"She passed away early this morning at the Lancaster," I replied, leaving out the fact that she was murdered.

"That's terrible! You know, I saw police cars over there, but I figured it was just a hotel issue. Poor dear."

"Isn't this great?" said Hudson from the stage. "Should I start singing 'Tiny Bubbles'?"

"Yes!" yelled an attendee in a different row.

I noticed everyone around us was sipping the first Champagne. I picked up mine and tasted it. The flavor was elegant and subtle, but overshadowed by the fact that Anita didn't know Jocelyn.

Anita downed the rest of her glass. "So good," she said.

"Agreed."

Hudson lifted the next one. "This second Champagne we're enjoying today is from Reims. The soil in the Champagne region is chalk, so if you get the opportunity to visit, be sure to go on a cellar tour. The long tunnels were carved by Romans centuries ago and you can still see the marks from the tools on the chalk walls. Anyway, I'm getting ahead of myself. Let's all enjoy." Hudson drank the glass, as did the rest of the audience.

I wanted to ask Anita more questions, but I needed to bide my time. I took a sip and smiled. "Do you like it?"

"Oh yes," said Anita as she finished the glass. "I love bubbles. They make me happy."

I nodded, eager to take advantage of the gap in Hudson's presentation. "Hey, what did you talk about in the lobby?"

"With who?"

"Jocelyn. She came over to talk to you last night."

"Did she?"

"She did," I replied. "I watched her." A nervous knot formed in my stomach. This was the only lead I had. If I was wrong, I was stuck.

"Oh, that," Anita finally said as she motioned with her hand to dismiss the incident. "That was just a quick hi and then she went to the restroom. We didn't talk."

"Are you sure?"

"Positive." She smiled.

"And you didn't know her? She said you were an old friend."

Anita laughed. "If old friend means a few hours, then shoot, we were old friends." She nudged me. "Heck, you and I are old friends, too!"

Sixteen:
Pairing Suggestion:
Chardonnay —
Adelaide Hills, Australia

Aged in oak, these elegant wines
are often overshadowed by
mass-produced ones.

When the seminar ended, Anita stood up and shuffled out of the row. I wanted to ask her more questions as I followed, but I didn't even know what to ask at that point. She said she didn't know Jocelyn and they didn't talk, but I had learned a lot about people from my years working in restaurants. The wave Jocelyn did was not a greeting to someone she just met. There was more to it, but I couldn't keep calling Anita's bluff. That wouldn't get me anywhere.

"That was fun!" said Anita as we reached the exit. "See you later, right?"

"Definitely," I replied. "Maybe we can even get drinks tonight."

"Count me in. That would be superb."

She gave a little wave as she walked away.

I leaned against the wall outside the ballroom, trying to think of what to do next, but I was distracted by a pacing figure. It was the nervous woman Dean and I encountered on the lawn. She was in a dark gray pantsuit and her long brown cascading curls were again pulled halfway up on her head like the day before, but her disposition seemed to be much worse. She looked like she was on the brink of tears. Had something happened or was she upset about the death? Did she know Jocelyn?

"Hey, are you okay?" I asked as I approached.

"Me?" Her voice went up with her breath. "Yes, I think so. Why?" She put her hand to the side of her face, her energy still nervous and jumpy.

"Sorry, I should have mentioned that we met yesterday. Outside on the lawn."

"Oh yes, that's right." She glanced around as if she had forgotten something. "Isn't there a seminar going on right now? I'm late. I should go."

"Are you okay?" I repeated one last time before she left.

"No." Tears formed in her eyes. "I don't like this. I just heard someone died this morning." She leaned closer. "Murdered," she whispered. "I want to go home. I don't like knowing a killer is on the loose."

"Wait, how did you hear it was murder?"

She put her hand to her mouth, as if she was biting her knuckles. "The other hotel had police cars," she said through her fingers. "Then in the last seminar, the people near me said a woman was murdered. What's happening?"

"It could be an isolated incident and have nothing to do with the festival." Even as I said it, I wasn't really sure. I didn't want to tell her that the body was found outside the festival emcee's door.

She looked at me. "Still, it happened here. I'm terrified. This is supposed to be a happy event and now someone's dead. I don't feel safe."

"Don't think of it that way. Focus on the wine and food. In fact," I said as I motioned to the nearby Stanley Ballroom, "let's go get a seat for the next seminar." I knew Hudson was hosting one, but I didn't mind which one we attended as long as she calmed down and felt better.

"I did want to go to the Rosé seminar, but that starts right now, and . . ." She pointed to the door and then shook her head. "Never mind, I need something stronger. Bar?"

I wasn't in the mood for a drink, but I didn't want to leave her on her own. "Sure."

We walked toward the hotel bar and I realized I didn't even know who she was. "Sorry, I didn't catch your name. I'm Katie Stillwell."

"Isabella Bernee." She smiled, but her eyes still darted around nervously, as if she was looking for the killer in every corner. In a way, I was too, though I was still interested in finding Jocelyn's real identity.

The bar was dark, even though it was daytime, because the whole room was covered with black marble, a stark change from the cozy antique bar at the Lancaster.

"Where would you like to sit?" I motioned to the tables. Nearly all of them were empty.

"Right at the counter," Isabella said as she walked to the far corner near the wall, pulled out a stool, and leaned on the cushioned edge of the bar.

I took the seat next to her as she looked around, her position giving her a view of the entire room, whereas I had my back to the place. She was like a scared animal, ready to jump up and run at any moment.

"Do you want me to choose a wine?"

"No," she exhaled. She focused her attention on the bottles on the back wall as the bartender waited. "I'll have a whiskey sour."

"One whiskey sour," said the bartender. "How about you?"

"Just water."

"Please." She put her hand on my arm. "I don't want to drink alone."

"Okay." I paused as I thought about what to order. "A German Riesling." They were lower in alcohol than most of the other wines on the menu.

Isabella let out a huge sigh, as if she was already relaxing, though nothing had really changed. A killer was still out there.

"Are you feeling better now?"

"No. Never. I was nervous about coming here already. I'm not a fan of crowds, and now this."

The bartender arrived with our orders.

Isabella lifted her glass and took a long drink. "Who was she?" she finally whispered.

"Who?"

"The woman who died."

I hesitated. I honestly didn't know anymore, but I could at least go with the name I had. The fake name. "Jocelyn Rivers."

Isabella's eyes grew wide with fear. "Jocelyn Rivers?"

"Yes. Did you know her?"

She put her hands to her face. "I talked to her. Yesterday." She lowered her palms onto the bar and took a deep breath, as if trying to calm herself.

"What did she look like?" I wanted to make sure she was talking about the Jocelyn who died and not the Jocie I met a few hours ago.

"I don't know, dark hair. Tall. She apologized for spilling wine on me at the seminar."

"Did she say anything else?"

Isabella bit her nails with her free hand while the other one grasped the whiskey sour. "We chatted briefly. She was having trouble. Something about wanting to connect with an old friend here, but was being ignored."

"Hudson? Anita?" I interjected but immediately regretted it. I needed to focus and not give all of my clues away.

"I don't know. She didn't say a name." Isabella drank more of her whiskey sour. "Should I be worried?"

"Worried about what?"

"The killer." Isabella knocked her glass, grabbing it as it tipped over, a splash of whiskey landing on my sleeve. "Sorry."

"It's okay." I dabbed at the spill and returned my focus to her. "I don't think you need to be concerned. You should focus on the festival."

"But there's a killer here. What if they come for me?" Isabella shook her head.

"Why would they come for you?"

"I don't know," she said as tears filled her eyes. "Why did they come for Jocelyn?"

SEVENTEEN:
PAIRING SUGGESTION:
POUILLY-FUMÉ —
LOIRE VALLEY, FRANCE

A Sauvignon Blanc wine with a
smoky characteristic.

Isabella was much calmer by the time she finished her drink. While I wanted to believe it was my influence, I knew the whiskey probably had more to do with it. Unfortunately, her question still lingered: Why did the killer come for Jocelyn? I wasn't sure, but I had a feeling Anita knew more. Hudson might, too.

"Thanks for talking with me," she said as she put her credit card on the counter. "Your drink is on me."

"No, it's okay."

"No," said Isabella with a stern tone. "You listened to me and we don't even know each other. I insist."

"Well, thank you," I replied. "That's very nice of you. Are you okay now?"

She looked around, still a little unsure of

everything. "I'm better."

"Are you going to stay for the rest of the festival?"

Isabella nodded. "I will. As long as nothing else happens."

"It won't," I replied, but even as I said it, I wasn't sure. I couldn't promise anything. Nothing about life was certain.

The bartender returned her card and Isabella put it away and stood up. She smoothed her hair held by the clip as she stared around the tables. "I wonder if they're in here."

"Who?"

She looked at me, the fear returning to her face. "The person who killed Jocelyn."

I shuddered but did my best to hide it from her. "Just focus on the festival." Though I knew I wouldn't be able to.

"I'll try," she replied as she took a deep breath. "I guess I'll see if I can catch the tail end of the Rosé seminar. Do you want to come?"

I glanced at the lobby sign for the events. "I might head to the one Hudson's hosting." If I could find him afterwards, I could ask if he knew Jocelyn's real identity. "But I'll see you later."

"Sure. Thanks again for sitting with me." She walked toward the exit. A waiter

157

brushed by her and she jumped, nearly knocking the tray out of his hand. Even the whiskey couldn't tame her nervous disposition. Perhaps the next wine seminar would take her mind off everything, but I knew it wouldn't for me.

I slid off the stool and headed toward the Whittier Ballroom.

The seminar was ending and patrons flowed out, some with glasses in their hands.

Hudson chatted with a young blond woman near the doors. He noticed me and nodded. I took the opportunity to approach him.

"Hudson," I said and glanced at the attendee next to him. "Sorry, didn't mean to interrupt."

She briefly touched his shoulder and stepped away.

"No, it's fine," replied Hudson. "She just came up to thank me for the seminar."

"Hey, how was it by the way?"

"Fantastic. We had some killer wines."

I shifted at Hudson's poor choice of phrasing. "I have a quick question for you. When Jocelyn Rivers came to your house last month, are you sure it was her?"

He stared at me with his eyebrows raised. "Of course."

"You actually talked to her face to face."

"No, my wife did. Sarah said some woman stopped by, talking about a wine company and then Jocelyn mentioned the visit at the opening ceremonies yesterday." Hudson stared across the lobby and I followed his focus. It was Anita.

"Do you know her?"

"Who? The redhead? No, but she looks nice. Listen, I gotta go. I have a winemaker dinner tonight, but maybe I'll see you for drinks later."

"Sure," I replied, but I didn't know when I would have the opportunity to talk to him alone again. "Just one last question."

"Good, 'cause I'm getting a little tired of them."

"Did Jocelyn hint about anything out of the ordinary last night? Like that she might not be who she said she was?"

"Who she said she was? She was Jocelyn."

"Yes, I know. But was there anything that seemed off? Maybe a comment she made?"

Hudson shrugged. "I don't know what you mean. She was happy to be here. She'd never been to a festival before and was excited to learn about wine."

"Anything else?"

"No, but she did say she needed me to meet her friend."

"Did you?"

"No, I stayed in the bar. Besides, I don't think she meant right then. I thought she just meant sometime during the weekend. I guess she was here with someone, but they weren't there last night. Tama . . ."

"Tama? Is Tama male or female?"

Hudson repositioned his stance as a look of annoyance crossed his face. "What's going on here? Are you interrogating me now, too?"

"No, sorry, that's not what I meant to do. I'm just trying to find out who did this so you're not under suspicion anymore. I'm sure you're still a suspect, you know. Even though you haven't been arrested. She was found outside your door."

Hudson stared at me with such intensity, it was as if he was calculating the probability of being arrested again. "Katie, I didn't kill her and I don't know who her friend was."

A cough came from behind us. It was Mr. Tinsley. "Mr. Wiley, a word."

"Gotta go," said Hudson. "Save your questions for someone else unless they're about the festival." He stepped over to Mr. Tinsley and as I looked around, even Anita was gone. I was alone. No Hudson, no Dean, and my only clue was the word *Tama,* which may or may not have to do with Jocelyn's real identity.

EIGHTEEN:
PAIRING SUGGESTION:
PINOT NOIR —
CASABLANCA VALLEY, CHILE

Grown in a cool climate, this wine
is very fruit forward.

I didn't have tickets to a wine dinner so I ate in the cafe at the New Sierra and returned to the Lancaster Hotel. A solitary police car was still parked out front and the stairs to the second level were cordoned off with yellow police tape, but the staff at the front desk were smiling, the bartender was serving drinks, and the attendant at the bell stand was ready to assist with bags. The hotel activity seemed back to normal.

I stared at the bellhop. Even though he wasn't the same one I had walked past the night before, it gave me an idea.

"Good evening," he replied. "Are you checking out? Do you need help with bags?"

"No, I'm looking for the bellhop who was here last night. Short dark hair, in his early twenties."

"Ah, you mean Eddie." He looked over his shoulder to the open door behind him. "Eddie, you have a fan."

Eddie walked out of the back room as the other attendant moved away. "Yes?"

"The woman who was found on the second floor . . ."

"Oh." His smile disappeared. "I'm sorry, but I'm not allowed to comment on that. All inquiries must be directed to our general manager," he said in rehearsed language.

"No, I'm not asking about that. Sorry, I should have started differently." I took a deep breath to try and fill my lungs, but they had tightened with my mistake. "Last night I was in the bar with a group, and I walked past you on the way out. Do you remember seeing us?"

"I don't know," he said slowly. "I'm not sure what I'm allowed to say. All inquiries —"

"Listen, don't say anything you don't want to, but I was over there in the bar with a group of six people that went down to four."

The bellhop stared at the ceiling as he thought about it. "Yes," he said as he snapped his fingers. "You were all near the fireplace."

"Exactly." I relished in the small victory. "There was a lady with dark brown hair and

162

a black dress with me. Does that sound familiar?"

"I think so."

"Perfect. Did you happen to talk to her at all yesterday? Perhaps when she arrived or when she met a friend in the lobby last night or maybe even later?"

"No," said the bellhop as he shifted nervously. "I'm not supposed to comment on our guests' activities. There's a whole privacy issue, you know?"

"I completely understand," I replied, unsure of how to proceed. I decided to go a more stealth route. "I'm just going to ask yes or no questions. All you have to do is reply yes or no and you don't have to tell me anything else."

The bellhop hesitated and glanced around, as if looking for an escape. "Yes, but make it quick. I need to be working."

"Do you know her name?"

"No."

"Did you see her meet someone in the lobby while we were all in the bar?"

"Yes."

"Was that person female?"

"Yes."

"Did she have red hair?"

He debated about it for a moment. "Yes."

"Did they chat for a while?"

163

"Yes. I think they talked for like, a minute or so, and then they both went to the bathroom."

"Together?" I *knew* Anita had been lying, and this just confirmed it.

He shrugged. "I don't know. Girls do that, don't they?"

"Okay, one last question. After I left the bar with my friend, the lady in the black dress stayed with the other gentleman we were with. Do you know how long she stayed after we were gone?"

He shook his head. "No. I don't remember the time, sorry. I only start watching the clock near the end of my shift."

"But you saw her leave?"

"Yes."

I leaned on the stand. "Did she go upstairs?"

"Yes."

"Was she alone?"

He looked at me and then away. "No."

"Was she with the red-haired lady you saw her talking to earlier?"

"No."

With the list of suspects dwindling, I had the sneaking suspicion that I already knew the answer to my next few questions. "Do you know the man she was with?"

"Yes," he replied as he dropped his voice

164

to a whisper. "The one who wears that big red pin."

"Hudson Wiley?"

"I don't know. I wasn't the one who took his bags to his room, I just remember seeing the pin."

As far as I knew, Hudson was the only attendee with the red MS pin at the festival, but just in case, I described him. With his hair, he was hard to mistake.

"Yes, that's him."

"Thank you, I really appreciate it."

"No problem. Let me know if I can be of any further assistance." He paused. "With your luggage, that is."

I nodded and stepped away. At least now I knew Anita had lied about talking to Jocelyn. It was nice to have confirmation on something. And she went upstairs with Hudson, which sort of confirmed his story, but not in a good way. However, there was still one more person I knew who had interacted with Jocelyn.

I walked into the bar area and felt a wave of relief as the same waiter was there, behind the counter this time.

"Hey," I said as I leaned on the bar. "Remember me? I was here last night."

He glanced up at me as he polished a glass with a white towel. "What would you like?"

"Not drinking, actually, I just have a question."

He didn't react.

"Okay then," I continued. "I was with the group by the fireplace and there was a lady with us. She had dark hair and wore a black dress and sat in that chair there." I pointed to the empty seat. "Did she pay by credit card?"

He continued to polish. "Don't know."

I debated for a moment, trying to see how I could find out more. "How about this, did you happen to see anyone else who might have talked to her besides Hudson?"

"I hear nothing and I see nothing," he replied with a smirk.

I knew where this was going. The young bellhop was hesitant to break the rules by talking to me, but this guy was playing a different game. I glanced around and then pulled out my wallet and put a five-dollar bill on the counter. He smiled but didn't move. I pulled out a ten and put it next to the five.

He stopped polishing and removed the two bills from the bar. "I don't listen to conversations. It gets too loud in here. But she spent the whole time with Hudson, except for that one lady."

"Which one?"

He picked up another glass. "Not sure. Some lady came up, started talking to her when Hudson left for a while."

"What did she look like?" I could barely contain my excitement. Either it was Anita, someone new who might know more, or it was the killer.

"Don't know. She had on a blue hat. One of those fancy ones. That's all I remember."

"A fancy hat?" The skepticism was clear in my voice. "I don't think I've seen a hat this entire festival." I looked around the bar and spotted Walt and Ben in the corner. I turned my attention back to the bartender to finish my questions. "Besides the hat, what else?"

"That's it. But their conversation was intense."

"You could hear it?"

"No, just the way she acted. Like professional and stuff. I see a lot of people doing business deals in here. Over drinks, you know? It seemed like it was one of those."

"And Hudson was part of it?"

He put the glass on the shelf. "She left before Hudson came back. He bought a few more drinks and that was that."

"Did any of them pay by credit card?" I repeated my earlier question, hoping that

167

the fifteen-dollar tip would now include that as well.

He shook his head. "Hudson covered the bill for your friend and then they left."

"Anything else?"

"If you're asking if I followed them out of the room, I didn't. I was working." His tone had shifted. "Speaking of." He turned his attention to a gentleman a few feet down the bar.

"I want a Negroni cocktail. Gin, vermouth, and Campari. *Capisce?*"

"You got it. Coming right up."

"Thanks for your help," I added, but he was busy making the cocktail. I directed my focus to Walt and Ben and walked over to their table. "Rick Roll, this seems to be your bar of choice."

"It's uncrowded," said Walt.

"And cozy and clever," added Ben.

"That doesn't make any sense," replied Walt. "How can a bar be clever?" He looked up at me, not waiting for Ben's answer. "Did you find your Beaujolais friend?"

"I did. Anita. Thanks for the tip earlier. What are you drink—" I stopped speaking as I stared at the label on the bottle of wine. It said *Tama Winery.*

"Merlot," replied Walt, but I was too busy processing the discovery. Tama wasn't a friend. It was a winery.

I swallowed hard and composed myself. "I didn't realize they had Tama on the list here."

"They don't."

"Watch out, Walt. She's going to challenge you to a taste test again."

"No, I'm not, but if it's not on the list, where did you get it?"

"A friend," replied Walt with a smile. "Keep the label turned this way. I don't want the bartender to see."

"Which friend?"

"Wouldn't you like to know?" Walt swirled his glass of Merlot.

"Yes, I would."

He shook his head and smiled. "My secret."

"No, I'm serious, I want to know."

"Sorry, Stillwell, I already gave you info today. I'm not sharing any secrets, especially when they involve free wine."

"Ooh, burn," said Ben. He looked at the bottle. "But if you'd like a glass, I'm sure Walt will share."

"I might. If I feel generous."

"No, that's okay." I thought about how to handle this. "Are they serving Tama at the festival events then?"

"Nope. It was a gift from a new friend,

and that's that." Walt motioned to the seat. "You're welcome to stay, but having you stand at the table is making me nervous." He took a drink. "Also, before you sit, you should know that I'm not going to answer the wine question no matter how long you stay. The subject is closed."

Ben lifted the bottle. "And almost empty."

I debated sitting but knew it wouldn't do any good. I wished them both good night and left the bar. Just like the row of wines I would have to identify at my upcoming exam, it seemed like multiple people at the festival had something to hide. And Tama Winery might be the key.

NINETEEN:
PAIRING SUGGESTION:
VERMENTINO —
SARDINIA, ITALY

A light white wine with an herbaceous
quality and a slightly bitter finish.

The next morning, I needed to clear my
mind and running was the way to do it. I
stuck to the main road and although there
weren't any vineyards near the hotel, the
scenery was calming and there wasn't much
traffic this early on a Saturday. Within an
hour or two, the streets would be busy with
people driving in for the festival or visiting
the nearby wineries, but I had woken up
early enough to miss that.

My late-night research on Tama Winery
had provided little information, only that it
was located farther up the coast and the
website was under construction. It might
mean nothing at all that Hudson mentioned
it and Walt and Ben had a bottle of it. Then
again, it might mean everything.

I ran along Mission Drive. The morning

sun highlighted the rolling hills and I looked forward to seeing the vineyards that would provide me with the calmness I needed.

I thought about the murder, Jocelyn's still-unknown true identity, and Anita lying about knowing her. I felt like I couldn't trust anyone, and maybe it was better that I didn't.

I turned down a side road and the vineyards came into sight, their organized rows providing relief to the tightness in my chest. Perhaps it was time to take a break from thinking over the events of the weekend and go over wine facts instead. With only three days until the test, this time was key. I didn't have my phone on me to look up flash cards, but I could recite the things I knew.

I chose the sizes of Champagne bottles and said them out loud in between breaths. "Demi, a half bottle. Standard bottle. Magnum, two bottles. Jeroboam, four bottles. Rehoboam, six bottles. Methuselah, eight bottles. Salmanazar, twelve bottles. Balthazar, sixteen bottles. Nebuchadnezzar, twenty bottles."

The number of cars on the road had increased. I didn't want to get hit by distracted drivers so I turned off onto a small one-lane street, which looked like it headed in the right direction back to the hotel.

Thick hedges lined both sides, but there was a cross street about a half mile away.

I decided to go over the major types of Italian sparkling wines next.

"Prosecco, Franciacorta."

A car turned onto the road behind me. I glanced back at it, a green sedan with dark windows, and returned my attention to my run.

"Lambrusco." I moved closer to the side of the road and waved the car on. "Asti Spumante."

It stayed behind me. A ball of uneasiness formed in my stomach and I increased my pace. There was room for the car to pass, but it was staying behind for some reason. I didn't know what it was, but I knew I didn't like it.

I focused on the cross street in the distance as I tried to go over wine answers, but the roar of the engine amplified as my lungs tightened.

Warning bells rang in my ears and I tried to glance back again. As I looked, the car lunged forward. It was trying to hit me.

I broke into a sprint, bringing my knees as high up as I could. I knew I couldn't outrun a car, but I had to try.

The cross street was still too far away and the thick row of bushes kept me on the pavement. I could feel the heat of the engine on the back of my legs. I was trapped.

My heart pounded and every muscle in my body tensed with adrenaline, but I kept running. The car continued the game, barely touching my heels as it stayed close.

If I slowed down, I might die. If I turned again to look at the car, I might die. I needed a way out and I looked for it with every step. Up ahead, the bushes seemed to break their uniformity. It was my only chance.

I sprinted with every last bit of energy I had, hoping that the variation in the hedge was a path and I could dive into it before the driver decided to end the game. And me.

Five feet to go.

The bumper touched the back of my legs.

Two feet to go.

I dove headfirst into the dirt between the bushes, tucking my feet up so they wouldn't meet the tires of the car. I waited for the car to crash over me as everything faded to black.

It didn't come.

The only sound was the squeal of the tires and the engine as it roared away. I scrambled up to get a look at the vehicle, but my foot caught and I fell back onto the dirt. By the time I got to the road, the green sedan was too far in the distance for me to see any distinguishing qualities or a license plate number.

My heart pounded and my whole body shook, but I didn't know if I had injuries, since shock could delay pain. I knew I had to get out of there in case the car came back.

I sprinted to the cross street and down the next block before I evaluated my arms and legs.

Scratches on my elbow and scraped knees from the dive into the dirt were the only evidence of the interaction. If the person had wanted to hit me, they would have.

This wasn't an attempted murder; this was a warning. Someone thought I knew something.

The question was who.

TWENTY:
PAIRING SUGGESTION:
CHARDONNAY —
SANTA BARBARA, CALIFORNIA

Aided by the fog, this region creates
excellent wines with balance and acidity.

I made it back to the Lancaster without
further incident. After I showered and put
Band-Aids on my cuts, I filed a police report
on the car. It didn't help that I didn't have
a description other than a dark green sedan,
but at least it was something.

I was tempted to text Dean about it, but I
didn't want to worry him, especially when
he was working and couldn't be with me. I
was okay and I was going to continue with
the festival, though my guard would be up.

The Chardonnay panel was about to start
as I hurried across the lawn. I always
enjoyed the stark difference between California Chardonnay and those from France,
such as Chablis, and the seminar was described as having both.

I walked into the ballroom. Walt and Ben

176

were in the fifth row with empty seats nearby. I wondered if either of them owned a green vehicle and since I was in a crowd of people, I decided it was safe to find out.

"How's your morning so far?" I sat down next to them. I wanted to ask if either of them had been for a drive, but I figured that would give too much away, so I stared at the six glasses of Chardonnay in front of me while I waited for a response.

"Someone's a little late," said Walt.

I glanced at my watch. "Actually, it doesn't start for four minutes. Some may say I'm not only on time, I'm early."

"Didn't mean you," replied Walt. He pointed to the front of the room where the three panelists waited on the stage. The space for the moderator was empty.

"Maybe Hudson drank too much last night," said Ben as he shrugged. "It happens."

"I wouldn't be surprised if he overslept," said Walt.

"Why should he get to oversleep? I didn't get to oversleep," replied Ben.

"Something isn't right," I said without meaning to say it out loud.

"Yes, we're missing the man of the hour," replied Walt.

The other panelists were starting to look

around, but I stared at the open space on the panel wondering if Hudson drove a dark green car. Why would he want to run me off the road?

"They might ask you to step in again," said Walt as he picked up a glass. "Are you ready to dazzle us with your knowledge?"

"I can read through this wine," said Ben as he held a glass of Chardonnay to the side.

Two festival officials on the far side of the room whispered to each other with their hands blocking their faces.

The taller one headed up to the podium. "We're going to start. Unfortunately, Hudson Wiley seems to be bit tardy, but we'll proceed and perhaps he'll join us later." He glanced at the panelists. "Michael, why don't you lead us for this one?"

The man sitting next to the empty seat looked surprised and then composed himself. "Okay, um, that's fine." He pulled the microphone in front of him closer. "Let's start with the first one, which happens to be mine. Um, my winery is located in Santa Rita Hills and we ferment in stainless steel. We strive to create bold yet unoaked Chardonnay."

I knew I couldn't sit there. What if Hudson was driving the car? Was he guilty and thought I was getting too close?

"I have to take a call," I whispered to Walt and Ben.

"I'm stealing your wine then," said Ben as he moved one of my glasses closer to his.

I pulled my phone out of my pocket and held it to my ear as I shuffled along the row and down the aisle, pretending I was on an important call.

I slipped outside the ballroom, making sure the door closed gently behind me. I didn't want to disturb the seminar more by a slamming door.

The hallway was empty except for a few stragglers heading to another ballroom, but I didn't want to know about the seminars. I wanted to know about the car. Specifically, Hudson's car.

I left the hotel and crossed the grass to the Lancaster valet stand.

"Name and room number," said the attendant, his focus on the computer.

"Actually, I'm not getting my car. I have a question." But I stopped. I was about to ask about Hudson's car, but maybe there was a different way to go. "I just want to make sure my car is still here."

The attendant narrowed his eyes. "Why would your car not be here?"

"Well, it's not mine, it's a friend's." The

lie didn't taste good as it came out of my mouth.

"I don't think I should get involved," said the attendant.

"Listen," I said as I stood in front of him. "You probably shouldn't. But all I need to know is if a certain someone's car is still here."

"Maybe you shouldn't be checking on your boyfriend's car."

"And maybe he's not my boyfriend and I just need to find out what car he drives." I put a five-dollar bill on the stand.

The attendant, probably still in college, hesitated for a moment and then took the money.

"Hudson Wiley, room two-oh-three. Wait, no, he changed rooms." The hotel had relocated him after Jocelyn's murder because the nearby hallway was still a crime scene. I didn't know his new room number.

"I don't think I'm breaking any rules by telling you Hudson Wiley drives a bright-red Porsche," said the attendant. "It's a pretty cool car and hard to miss. However, I'm not sure I can tell you if it's still here."

"No, that's fine," I replied as a mixed wave of relief and remaining questions went through me. "You've already told me all I needed to know." At least now I knew it wasn't Hudson who tried to hit me.

"Good luck with your, um, relationship with Mr. Wiley," said the attendant.

"Yeah, not my boyfriend."

"Got it."

I stepped away from the attendant and paused as I glanced through the window to the Lancaster Hotel's front desk. It was worth it to cover one more base before I left.

A woman in her twenties was behind the front desk, her black hair pulled back in a French twist. "Good morning," she said. "What can I help you with?"

"Morning. I'm looking for Hudson Wiley. He's a guest here. About six-one with a lot of hair."

"Yes, I know Mr. Wiley." She smiled.

"Great. Do you happen to know where he is?"

"He walked through the lobby about an hour ago, on his way to the festival at the New Sierra, I believe."

"So he left here and walked over?"

She tilted her head. "Yes, there would be no reason to drive over to the New Sierra. Is there an issue?"

"No, not at all. I was just looking for him. He was late to a seminar. He's probably already there."

She nodded and returned her focus to the computer.

I walked back to the New Sierra Hotel. The lobby and conference area were calm, with only a few attendees milling about and no officials running around, trying to solve an issue. Maybe Hudson really was back. Maybe he had been waylaid by a meeting or lost time chatting to an attendee and was now leading the seminar. Everything was probably fine.

I cracked open the door to the Chardonnay seminar. There was an empty seat in the last row, which I could take without making a disturbance. I crept in and sat down before looking at the panel.

Hudson was still missing.

TWENTY-ONE:
PAIRING SUGGESTION:
ZWEIGELT —
KREMSTAL, AUSTRIA

A light red wine with low tannins and
notes of cherry and cinnamon.

I stayed the rest of the seminar, as I didn't want to cause another disruption by leaving it twice. Although it was educational and I tried to concentrate on the different types of Chardonnay that ranged from buttery California ones to unoaked French examples with more acidity, my mind was preoccupied by Hudson's absence.

When the seminar ended, I moved out of my row, meeting Walt in the aisle.

"Glad to see you made it back," he said. "Ben here drank all your wine."

"Did not," said Ben as he put his chin up. "Only some of it."

I smiled in response, but my eyes were already scanning the exit for Hudson. I made my way outside the ballroom, where the attendees milled around like nothing was wrong. And perhaps nothing was, but Hudson had been upset that he missed the Pinot seminar when he was questioned. To miss two seminars in one weekend wasn't just out of character, it was suspicious. Maybe he had been called back in for questioning.

I kept my eyes on the crowd instead of looking at the booklet for the lunch location. Every face walking past was unfamiliar. Until one wasn't.

It was Dean.

His smile was huge, but he breathed heavily as if he'd run all the way from Los Angeles. "I made it," he said, his eyes glistening. "I didn't think I would, but I got here in time."

I grinned. "Does that mean you sped here? Do I need to write you a ticket?"

"Not today. I obeyed the speed limit. Did you get my texts?" His smile increased.

I reached for my phone. "Sorry, I didn't even look."

"No, it's fine. I'm used to you not having your phone, though you actually do have it."

"I'm still not used to checking it," I replied, even though I had taken it out during the seminar as the ruse to leave. I never liked carrying my phone around and being accessible at all times, but an incident earlier in the year had prompted me to bring it more often.

"It was just to let you know that I was on my way." Dean glanced at his watch. "But we need to start walking to make it in time."

"In time for what?"

"Your surprise. Did you forget?"

"No." But I did forget. With everything going on, the surprise had been the furthest thing from my mind. "I'm excited."

"Great, let's go."

We walked past the ballrooms, but I continued to scan the crowds for Hudson.

"Everything okay?" asked Dean.

"Of course. Just curious." I didn't want to tell him that Hudson was missing and a car had tried to run me down. Or that the murder victim might have been using a stolen name and festival pass. At least not yet. He was too excited about the surprise and I didn't have the heart to dampen his smile right then. "So where exactly are we going? You mentioned it was wine related, so . . ." I motioned to the festival. "Is it a special meeting with one of the chefs? Or a winemaker?"

"Nope." He looked at his watch again. "In fact, we need to walk a little faster."

"Is it at the other hotel?"

"Not quite." Dean held open the front entrance to the New Sierra.

I stepped out and noticed his car near valet. "It's a drive?" I looked at him. "What are you up to, Dean?"

"You're about to find out. Valet has my keys, I'll be right back."

I smiled as he walked away but noticed Isabella to the side.

"Isabella?" I said gently.

She jumped as she turned to look at me. "Sorry, I wasn't expecting to hear my name."

"You okay?"

"Oh yes. Just waiting for my car." She smiled, but it was a weak one. "I thought I might get some food in town."

"But you're continuing with the festival, right?"

"Yes, I'm coming back later." She still looked a little timid. "You were right. It's fun. I'm glad I stayed."

"I'm glad, too. Hey, by the way, have you seen Hudson?"

Her eyes grew wide. "Who's that?"

"The Master Sommelier who's the master of ceremonies this weekend. He's pretty tall and wears a bright red pin."

"The hair guy," she replied.

"Sure," I said as I stifled a laugh. "The

186

hair guy. Have you seen him today?"

"No, why?" She put her hand to her mouth. "What's going on?" She looked like she was on the brink of tears again and there wasn't any whiskey to help this time.

"I'm sure he's fine, I just missed him earlier." Though even as I said it, I didn't believe it was true.

Isabella stared at me.

"Katie, you ready?" said Dean as he stood at the open door to his car.

"I'm sure he's fine," I said again to Isabella. "Enjoy your lunch and when you get back, he'll be at the festival."

She glanced around with jerky movements, as if she couldn't take in what was happening. I didn't know if she should be driving in that condition, but it might be her permanent disposition.

"A new friend of yours?" asked Dean as I got into the car.

"She's the one you scared on the lawn the other night."

"Ah, yes. Is she okay?"

"I think so. I'll fill you in a little later. Let's enjoy the day first."

"Looks like I'm not the only one with surprises." He smiled.

"Something like that. So," I said, wanting to focus on my time with Dean, "do I get to know where we're going now?"

"You'll know soon enough," he said as he drove out of the hotel. "But I guarantee it will be an adventure."

An adventure just like a missing Master Sommelier and almost being run over that morning?

"Can't wait," I replied.

Twenty-Two:
Pairing Suggestion:
Moscato d'Asti —
Piedmont, Italy

A lighthearted, sweet, and
slightly sparkling wine.

We drove through Solvang, a Danish village
known for its architecture, Christmas stores,
and a windmill in the middle of the town.

"Are we stopping in Solvang?"

"No," said Dean. "But maybe we'll come
back for lunch."

He continued driving and I stared out at
the golden hills of Santa Barbara County.
Oak trees dotted the slopes but no vineyards. At least not yet.

We reached the freeway.

"You're not driving me back to San Francisco, are you? Or down to L.A.? I mean, I
know you just went there, but I'm not ready
to go."

Dean smiled as he passed the entrance to
Highway 101. "This is a good surprise, I
promise. Nothing to do with your father."

"Did you see him down there?"

"No. I would tell you if I had."

I knew Dean had met him once, but that was way before he met me and knew the history and tension between us. "And the Harper case? Did you get what you needed?"

"Somewhat. I might have to go to L.A. again on Monday, but at least I'm able to join you today. It's important for me to do this for you."

"For me?" I stared at him, hoping for a clue. "Does it involve a winery? Or a wine shop? A vineyard?"

He laughed. "I can hear the anticipation in your voice. You're not one for surprises, are you?"

"I'm used to logic and planning. I would think you would be, too, Detective."

"A few more minutes. Patience."

"You know that's not my strong point." I returned my gaze out the window. There were vineyards along the road now, their organized lines instilling calmness within me. I took a deep breath, the scenery already soothing out the events of the morning. The vines were full of grapes, soon to become wine and perhaps even served in Trentino one day. We had several wines from Santa Barbara on the wine list.

The car slowed at a driveway next to a colorful sign with the name Bartlett.

"We're going to Bartlett?"

"You know it?"

"Yes, it's on our wine list," I replied as my mind went into its factual mode that I used at the restaurant. "Bartlett is known for their Chardonnay, Pinot Grigio, Pinot Noir, and Merlot. It was founded in 1970 by William Bartlett Junior but he sold it in the 1990s." I hoped my memory would be this sharp at Tuesday's exam.

"I'm impressed," said Dean. "As I mentioned on Thursday, the owner is a family friend from a long time ago. When I found out we were coming to the festival, I made a few calls."

"Are we doing a tasting?"

"You'll see," said Dean.

"You're so mysterious today. It's kinda fun."

We drove toward a gray single-story building that seemed to sink into the ground and a wood barn next to it. As we got closer, the top of two staircases appeared as they spiraled into a sunken courtyard below the front of the building. A Chocolate Labrador ran out of the barn as we parked.

"That's Caleb," said Dean. "He has a big bark but he's a sweetheart." I stayed in the car as Dean approached the dog. "Hi, Caleb. It's me."

The Lab continued to guard the barn, barking furiously. Not that I wasn't a fan of dogs, but an unknown dog defensively showing its teeth? No thanks.

"I know it's been a long time, but you've met me before." Dean put out his hand and let Caleb sniff it. The barking stopped and the wagging started. "Good to see you, Caleb. I'm glad you remember me."

I opened the car door. Dust and dry earth permeated the air, but there was still the aroma of fermenting grapes.

An older man with a straw hat, white shirt, and jeans appeared from the steps of the sunken building. "Johnny Dean, I figured that was you since Caleb stopped barking. I'm glad you made it in time. I almost gave up on you guys."

"Sorry, work got in the way. Are we too late?"

"You just caught me, so we're all good."

"Thanks, Frank." Dean shook his hand. "It's great to see you again. I know it's been a while."

"You should visit more often. I told your mom she should come see me, too."

"She will." Dean motioned to me. "Frank, this is Katie."

"Pleasure to meet you." He was in his late sixties and his gray hair stuck out in tufts beneath his hat. "I hear it's a special occasion for you," he said as I shook his weathered hand.

I looked at Dean and back at Frank. "I don't even know what we're doing yet."

"Ah, he didn't tell you." He waved toward the barn. "Come around to the back. Let's get you started."

Dean took my hand and we followed Frank to a covered gray plastic tub, approximately five feet by five feet.

"There you go!" said Frank.

"I'm still not following."

He lifted the cover to reveal mounds of green grapes that filled the tub.

I wasn't sure how to process the sight.

"Haven't you seen grapes before?" Frank laughed and his whole body convulsed. "Kidding. This is what Johnny said you wanted."

"Grape stomping," said Dean as he put his arm around me. "When I knew we were coming to Santa Barbara, I called Frank and told him I had a special person in my life who had wanted to stomp grapes ever since she saw that episode of *I Love Lucy*. He managed to pull a few strings and set this up for us."

I stared into Dean's blue eyes as my whole body filled with emotion. I told him about my wish to go grape stomping when we were at Garrett Winery last fall, but I was pretty sure I hadn't mentioned it since. "You remembered," I managed to say, my voice soft and halting.

"Of course."

"I don't know what to say."

"Don't say a thing," said Frank. "Get in the tub and start stomping." He sat down on another crate in the shadow of the barn, Caleb faithfully at his feet.

I slipped off my boots and rolled my black pants up, the cuffs stopping slightly below my scraped knees.

Dean did the same with his jeans and held out his hand. "Ready?"

"Definitely." I held his arm as I stepped into the tub, the cold grapes crushing under my feet with my first step. "One just popped between my toes!"

Dean climbed in next to me. "It's cold."

"Start stomping, you kids," yelled Frank from the side. "Those grapes aren't going to squash themselves!"

I lifted up my knees as juice, seeds, and skins lodged between my toes with every step. The feeling was unlike anything I had ever felt before. Grapes continued to pop under my feet and I couldn't stop laughing.

I glanced at Dean. He had a huge smile on his face as he watched me while he stomped but with a quarter of the effort.

"You're pretty good at this," shouted Frank. "Sure you haven't done this before?"

"Never," I replied. "But you aren't going to use these grapes for your wine, are you?"

"Sure, we love the essence of feet," said Frank, followed by a hearty laugh. "Nah, these aren't even my grapes. They're from a vineyard up the road. Didn't ripen properly. They look ripe on the outside, but they're still young on the inside. Can't make wine out of 'em, so why not squash 'em for fun!"

I stomped harder, juice squirting up my legs, spraying juice and skins everywhere. Soon the entire tub had turned into a mass of liquid that hid our ankles and feet.

"I think they're all done," I said as I moved through the pulpy liquid. "I can't find any more grapes." I looked up at Dean and laughed. "How did seeds get on your face?"

"Someone, and I won't say who, was very energetic in their stomping," said Dean. He took out a handkerchief and wiped his cheek. "I don't think I've ever seen you so happy."

"I haven't had this much fun in a long

time." I stepped forward. "Wait, I think I found another grape to squash." I moved my foot around. "Shoot, it floated away."

"Looks like soup to me," said Frank. "But don't let me stop ya. You're welcome to stay in there as long as you want."

I splashed around a little bit more and then stopped. "Okay." I could barely speak, my cheeks aching from the smiling. "I think I got all of them."

"So you're good? All done?" asked Dean.

I nodded as I stepped around one last time to make sure there weren't any remaining grapes.

"There's a mat on the side of the tub — unless you want juice mixed with dirt, then by all means, go onto the dirt," said Frank.

I stepped onto the faded blue mat and made room for Dean.

Frank turned on a hose. "Let me wash that stuff off. It gets sticky real fast." Grape skins flew to the ground as he sprayed down our feet. When all remnants were gone, he shut off the hose and tossed me a towel.

"Thanks." I wiped off my feet and gave the towel to Dean. I rolled down the cuffs of my pants back to my ankles. Dean's pants had survived the experience without noticeable grape residue, but a thick layer of juice had soaked into mine.

"Thanks, Frank," said Dean. "Can we help you clean up?"

"Not a chance." He pulled the cover on the tub. "I gotta run, so I'll take care of this tomorrow. You guys go have fun."

"Thank you so much," I said to Frank. "This was perfect. Truly perfect."

"It was all because of that guy right there." Frank pointed at Dean.

"Thank you, Johnny." I winked.

"Ah, Dean is fine." He beamed. "Was it a good surprise?"

"The best. I don't think anyone has ever done something so special for me."

Dean leaned forward and pulled a squashed grape out of my hair. "I'm not sure how this got up here, but it did." He was only a few inches away from me and his blue eyes glistened in the midday sun.

"Thank you, Dean."

His gaze focused to an intense and deep stare into my eyes.

My heart rate climbed.

He leaned closer and touched my cheek with his hand.

We both waited, neither one moving, as our surroundings faded away and we reduced the remaining gap. My eyes closed instinctively as his warm lips met mine. The world was silent and the moment was just for us until I heard Frank and Caleb stir nearby.

I opened my eyes and stepped back.

Dean had a strange smile on his face as if he was both happy and embarrassed. He took my hand. "Let's get lunch before we head back to the festival. You can tell me all about the panels that I missed."

"Ah, yes. I actually have a lot to fill you in on."

TWENTY-THREE:
PAIRING SUGGESTION:
RIESLING —
FINGER LAKES, NEW YORK

The lakes cool the vineyards in summer
and protect them from harsh winters.

We chose a restaurant not far from the hotel
and were seated at a window table.

"We should have a glass of wine," said
Dean as he looked over the lunch menu.

"It's midday. Who are you?" I smiled, but
I'd never known Dean to drink in the
middle of the day, even if it was a weekend.

He shrugged. "It makes sense after the
grape stomp."

"I'm glad you weren't keen on drinking
the grapes we squashed."

"Do people do that?"

I laughed. "I wouldn't say it's recom-
mended." I glanced at the menu for the
wines, but they weren't listed.

"What's everyone thinking for drinks?"
asked the waiter as he arrived.

I wanted to reply that I was thinking about

the location of the wine list, but I decided to be more tactful. "We'd like to order wine. Which ones do you have?"

"Oh, we have all the colors," the waiter remarked.

I paused, not sure how to respond.

"I think she'd still like a wine list," added Dean.

"Of course." His smile was close-lipped and he walked away.

"Thank you," I whispered to Dean. "That just kind of shocked me."

"Not a problem. Maybe he's new?"

"Maybe."

The waiter returned a moment later with the wine list and placed it in front of Dean. I took a deep breath and kept my mouth shut. I decided not to treat it as an insult, but as an oversight from the waiter.

Dean handed it to me. "Why don't you choose a wine for both of us?"

I ordered a glass of Sauvignon Blanc for Dean and a Viognier for myself. The waiter took the menu and retreated.

"So tell me," said Dean. "What did I miss?"

"Right." I took a deep breath. "First off, I'm fine, but I had a little incident with a car this morning. I went for a run and one nearly hit me."

"You're kidding."

"I wish I was, but don't worry, I filed a police report."

Dean's face was ashen. "Was it on purpose? Why didn't you tell me earlier?"

"You were so excited for the surprise. I didn't want to ruin it. I knew it could wait until now and I'm okay. In fact, I'm great. I just stomped grapes."

Dean slowly nodded, but I could tell he was still processing the information.

I leaned forward. "I'm fine. I would tell you if I wasn't. Okay, next up," I said to change the conversation. "I met Jocie Rivers."

"Yes, in the bar on Thursday night. I was with you." Dean raised his eyebrows. "Did you hit your head during the car incident?"

"No, I didn't, and I'm not talking about that Jocelyn Rivers. I met the real Jocie Rivers. She's in her sixties and is at the festival with some friends. She goes by Jocie, which is short for Jocelyn. She lost her badge just minutes after she got there on Thursday."

Dean stared at me, his expression transformed into disbelief. "Jocie Rivers. Jocelyn Rivers."

I nodded. "And I don't believe in a coincidence that two people with the same name are at the festival."

"If she's Jocelyn Rivers," continued Dean, "who did we have drinks with? Who was murdered?"

"I don't know."

"Did you tell the police?"

I swallowed hard. "No. What if I'm wrong? Besides, you told me not to get involved."

"And you listened?"

I shrugged. "For the most part. I might have tried to find out who she really was."

"Did you?"

"Not yet."

The waiter arrived with the two glasses of white wine except mine had a straw. It bobbed in my glass of Viognier and I tried to decide if the idea of drinking something as elegant and revered as wine out of straw was worse than knowing the plastic was possibly imparting synthetic flavors.

"Um," I finally said as I stared at the glass in front of me.

"Ah," replied the waiter. "One moment." He pulled out the straw and tapped it on the side to shake loose any remaining wine before tucking it behind his back. "Sorry about that. It was so I could tell them apart. You don't want to drink your wine through a straw."

"No, I really don't," I replied.

"We'll need a few more minutes on the

food," said Dean.

"I'll be back to take your orders." He smiled and walked away as I continued to comprehend the idea of a straw in my wine.

"Well, that was a first," I said.

"I bet you'd never do that at Trentino," remarked Dean.

"Not a chance. I'd never do that any-where."

Dean held up his glass. "Here's to grape-stomping adventures with my favorite part-ner in crime."

"Or favorite partner in fighting crime?"

"You make us sound like superheroes."

I shrugged. "Well, if it works." We clinked the glasses. "Cheers."

I watched as Dean tried the local Sauvi-gnon Blanc I ordered for him. "Do you like it?"

He nodded. "I almost get lemon in there. Is that correct?"

"Yes! Want to try one more?" I reached for his glass. "May I?"

"Of course."

I took a sip. "Okay, see if you can also find the peach in there, specifically white peach."

Dean tasted it again. "Definitely."

"Really?"

"No, not yet." He looked at the wine. "But I'll keep trying."

I grinned at him. "You'll be blind tasting in no time."

"Thanks, but I'll leave that up to you. Your skills are impressive." Dean smiled. "How has the studying been this weekend?"

"Not as much as I planned. With everything that's been happening, I was a little distracted, but I'll find some time."

Dean nodded. "Is Hudson still acting suspicious?"

"Well, that's another thing," I said as I took a deep breath. "He's kind of missing."

"Katie, what's going on?"

"I don't know." I flipped my fork over and over on the placemat as my lungs tightened. "All I know is that Hudson wasn't at the seminar this morning. He was supposed to host it and he was a no-show."

"It's possible he skipped town. Did you fill in for him?"

"No, one of the other panelists did. I made sure his car was still there, which it was, and the front desk at the Lancaster said they'd seen him in the lobby an hour before. Maybe the police were questioning him again?"

"That's an easy thing to find out." Dean stared at me. "I wonder if he knew Jocelyn wasn't who she said she was."

"He didn't seem to when I asked him

about it, but he did mention that Jocelyn was at the festival with someone and then he said the word Tama."

"Tama?"

"Yes, and last night Walt and Ben were drinking a bottle from Tama Winery. They wouldn't tell me where they got it, but I have a feeling it's the key to everything."

"When we get back, you'll figure it out."

"Why do you say that?" I asked.

"I'm starting to know you better than you think. You can't resist a mystery."

"Does that bother you?"

Dean smiled. "No. I'm just glad I'm back up here with you."

"I am, too."

"Are we ready to order now?" asked the waiter.

I glanced at the menu. "I think so." But even as I looked at the food choices, I thought about the festival. Though I hoped Hudson was back and everything was running like normal, I had the distinct feeling it wouldn't be.

TWENTY-FOUR:
PAIRING SUGGESTION:
AGIORGITIKO —
NEMEA, GREECE

A red wine with high acidity and tannins.

The lobby of the Lancaster was quiet, with most guests out for the day either attending the seminars or touring the nearby towns of Los Olivos, Ballard, and Buellton.

"Did you want to change before we return to the seminars?"

I looked down at the seeds stuck to the cuffs of my pants. "I think that's a good idea."

"Wait, Ms. Stillwell," said Mr. Tinsley from the side of the front desk, his hand up to signal us. He continued to talk on his cell phone as we approached. "No, I've been calling three-oh-three. I told you, no one is answering." He put the phone flat against his suit jacket. "Have you seen Mr. Wiley? We can't find him and his phone goes straight to voicemail."

"He's still missing?" My gut feeling had

been right.

"What do you mean *still* missing?" Mr. Tinsley's eyebrows went up as far as they could go.

"He wasn't at the seminar this morning," I replied.

"I knew it, I knew it." Mr. Tinsley shook his head as his voice escalated. "They tried to cover for him, but it's no good. Hiring him for this festival was a mistake. A rather unfortunate mistake."

"He could be in police custody," said Dean.

"That would be the icing on the cake," said Mr. Tinsley. "A festival brought to a halt because the host is under arrest."

"It may be something else," I added. I had a growing feeling of unease that Hudson was in trouble.

"Sure," said Mr. Tinsley, his voice reflecting that he was anything but sure. "People can't keep covering for him. This is ridiculous. He's missed more seminars than he's hosted at this point. If you find Mr. Wiley, tell him I need to see him immediately." He put the phone to his ear and stormed across the lobby.

"Dean, what if Hudson's disappearance is connected to the murder? And I don't just mean being questioned."

"You know him better than I do. Maybe he's drinking with friends?"

I shook my head. "I only met him when you did, but something's off here. Even the director of the festival doesn't know where he is." I glanced down at the grape seeds on my pants. "I'm going to change and then we'll see if there's more to the story over at the New Sierra."

Dean looked around. "I'll find out if he's in custody. Meet you back here."

I went to the elevator but instead of reaching for the second floor button, I found myself pushing the one for the third floor, where Hudson had been relocated after the murder. Thanks to Mr. Tinsley, I now had his new room number.

Nerves pulsed through me, but I tried to convince myself it was worth it just to make sure he wasn't in his room. I knocked on 303.

No response.

I knocked again.

A housekeeper pushed a cart at the end of the hallway.

"Excuse me," I called to her. "Can you open up a room for me?"

She nodded and walked down the hallway, but paused before she used the key. "Is it your room?" she asked.

"No," I replied with my knee-jerk honesty. Why did I do that? "It's my friend's room and I just want to check on him."

"I can't open it if it's not your room."

"I just need to make sure he's not in there. It's a safety issue. In fact," I added, "how about you go in there and check? There's nothing wrong with that, right?"

She debated for a moment before knocking on the door. "Housekeeping." She unlocked the door and I stepped forward. "No, you have to stay out here." She went inside as I waited in the hallway. I tried to peer through the doorway but couldn't see anything.

"It's empty," said the housekeeper.

"Empty like he's checked out?"

"No, his clothes and suitcase are in the room, but he's not." She closed the door behind her.

"Thank you."

At least I knew he wasn't in there passed out, or worse. I went to my room, changed, and returned to the lobby.

"Katie," said Dean as he walked toward me with efficiency.

"Hey. Did you find out if he's in custody?"

"He's not, but they've identified Jocelyn." He motioned to the floor above. "Her real name was Rachel Carlson. She's from Santa

Barbara and works in a fitness center."

"So not in wine at all?" I stared at the floor as the information turned in my mind. "Why did she pretend to be Jocelyn Rivers?" I put my hand up before Dean could speak. "I'm guessing it was just to have the pass. But why did she want to talk to Hudson about a wine company?"

"I don't know," said Dean. "And unfortunately, we can't ask her."

"Now I'll share my news. Hudson isn't in his room and he hasn't skipped town — or if he has, he left all his stuff."

Dean stared at me. "Where did you hear that?"

"I have my sources and you have yours."

He gave me a skeptical look. "You said you weren't going to get involved."

"Have you met me? When I went to change, I decided to check that his belongings were still in his room."

"How?" Dean's face was stoic.

"Nothing illegal, I promise. I had housekeeping check. Come on, let's go over to the New Sierra." I wanted to divert the attention from me doing potentially shady things. Dean knew I sometimes bent the rules. He had even arrested me last year after a winery owner pressed charges, but they were dropped long before we started dating. Now I was law-abiding, or at least tried to be.

Dean held the door open as we left the hotel. "I still don't understand why you're not in law enforcement."

"I told you. It's complicated."

"I know you didn't graduate from the Police Academy, but you could have tried again."

I shook my head. "My passion is wine."

"And solving things with wine."

"Except right now that's not helping find Hudson. I want to know where he is . . ." I paused. "Where do we find a missing somm?"

"The wine cellar? Sorry, I don't mean to joke about it, but it seems like the logical place," said Dean. "Where else could someone hide a body?"

"A body?" My heart fell. "Please don't tell me you think he's dead."

"It's a possibility," replied Dean.

As much as I didn't want to agree with him, he was right. There was a chance that whoever killed Rachel had already taken care of Hudson. We might be too late.

Twenty-Five:
Pairing Suggestion:
Salice Salentino —
Puglia, Italy

A very drinkable red wine made from
the Negroamaro grape.

I kept an eye out for Hudson as we walked across the grass. I had a small amount of hope that Mr. Tinsley had located him in the last few minutes, though I knew it was unlikely.

"Look, it's my favorite seminar leader," said Jocie — the real Jocie Rivers — as she approached with two of her friends. "This is the Katie I was telling you about," she said as she glanced at them. "They missed your seminar yesterday, but I told them all about it."

"I'm so bummed we missed your talk on Pinot," said one of her friends. "Are you going to give another one?"

"She doesn't know yet," said Jocie, answering for me. She looked at Dean. "Who's this tall drink of water?"

"Dean," he said as he put out his hand. Jocie shook it, as did the other two ladies, who then smiled and winked at each other.

Jocie leaned close to me and put her hand at the side of her mouth. "He's a cutie. Nice catch." She wasn't as quiet as I would have liked, and one of her friends giggled.

"I hope you had a nice time at the other seminars," I quickly added to ease the awkwardness. I avoided eye contact with Dean. I didn't know if he was smiling or embarrassed.

"We did!" exclaimed one of the ladies. "I learned that wine starts to turn to vinegar the moment you open the bottle so you have to drink it fast. I'm good at that."

"And Silvia here learned how to taste wine like a pro."

"You suck air across the wine in your mouth like this." Silvia put her lips together and breathed in. "You get more of the flavors that way. I'm going to call it the canary, 'cause it sounds like a bird singing when I do it."

"Canary," replied Jocie. "Ain't she a hoot!"

"I think canaries chirp, actually," said Silvia. "Not that I have one at home, that is. I just know it."

"Where is home?" asked Dean.

"Los Angeles! We're up here for a girls' weekend."

"That sounds fun," I replied.

"You have no idea," said Jocie as she laughed, her guest pass flapping in the wind. "We're getting wild!"

"Woo!" the two other ladies responded in unison.

I glanced at her pass. If there was more of a reason for Rachel to take the original pass from her other than gaining entrance to the festival, I wanted to know what it was. "Do any of you work in the wine world?"

"The wine world?"

"I mean, what do you do? For work?"

"Oh sweetie, we're all retired."

"But did any of you work in the wine industry, perhaps at a winery or a distributor?" I asked.

"No, but I drank a lot of it," said one of them.

"Me, too. Does that count?" said another.

I smiled. "Absolutely." They were so sweet together. I wanted to attend wine and food festivals with friends like them. "One last question, have any of you heard of Tama Winery?"

"No, is that a good one?" asked Jocie. "Should I add it to my shopping list?"

"I'm not sure yet." I glanced at Dean.

"But listen, have a wonderful day and enjoy the festival."

"Let me know if you do another seminar, okay?" Jocie pointed at me. "We want to sit in the front row."

"I'll save you three seats."

"Woo-hoo," replied Jocie, and the three of them continued into the hotel.

"Nice ladies," said Dean.

"I agree. They're here to have a good time, which means that Rachel just took the opportunity of a lost pass to assume her identity. Hudson never said Jocelyn's name in reference to the visit at his house in Denver, only that she mentioned it at the opening ceremonies so he knew it was her. The question is, why did someone who works at a fitness center want to talk to Hudson about a winery?"

"The question at the moment though —"

"Is where is Hudson," I interrupted. "Come on."

We entered the New Sierra as crowds flowed out of the ballrooms with the release of the last seminar of the day.

Walt and Ben strolled through the lobby, each with a glass of wine.

"Hey, the famous duo is back together again," said Walt. "Why aren't you drinking?"

"Just got back, haven't had a chance to get any wine yet," I replied.

"Got back? Where did you guys go?"

"Grape stomping," replied Dean.

"No way," said Ben. "They have that here?" He looked around the lobby. "Where? I want to go."

"No, it was a special event at a winery," I added. "Sorry."

Ben looked heartbroken at the news. Clearly I wasn't the only one who had dreamed of stomping grapes. "First it's a weird day and now I've missed grape stomping. What next?"

"Define weird day," said Dean.

"Apparently Hudson is playing hooky," said Walt. "Didn't host a single seminar."

"Probably off boozing it up," added Ben. "Then Walt here broke two glasses."

"This one's still intact," said Walt as he held up his glass.

"You should win a prize," replied Ben.

"So you haven't seen Hudson at all today?" I asked.

"Nope. Too busy watching Walt break his glasses," said Ben.

Walt knocked the glass out of Ben's hand. It landed on the carpet and a large shard broke off. "Nearly even."

Dean shifted next to me. "Okay, then."

He picked up the pieces.

Ben glared at Walt. "That was rude and uncalled for. Not only do you now owe me a drink, you're paying for dinner. Just watch, I'm going to get the biggest steak on the menu."

"Lovely," replied Walt. "At least I don't have to buy you dinner here. I can find somewhere cheaper."

"Why not here?" I asked.

"We heard a busboy say management lost the keys to the food storage and the restaurant might not open tonight. I tell ya, if there ever was a day to drink, this is it." Walt pointed to our empty hands. "I see you don't agree. I think it's bar time."

"Yes, bar time," added Ben. "Then we can figure out where Walt's buying me a steak dinner."

I smiled but my thoughts were still on the comment from the busboy. "We'll have to catch you a bit later. We have to go see about something."

"Agreed," said Dean as he stepped away with me. We locked eyes.

"Restaurant?" I said.

"Restaurant," he replied.

Twenty-Six:
Pairing Suggestion:
GSM Blend —
Paso Robles, California

Made from Grenache, Syrah, and
Mourvèdre, this Rhône blend has a
bold yet earthy quality.

The door was unlocked even though the
restaurant didn't officially open for two
hours. We passed by the tables and stopped
in front of the kitchen. Food prep started
early in the day and I didn't want to barge
in.

"Aren't you going in?" asked Dean.

"It's kind of trespassing, kind of uncool to
walk into the kitchen. Not to mention the
whole food safety thing. Besides, we don't
exactly have probable cause yet."

"You're definitely a cop's daughter,"
replied Dean.

"I'm sure a waiter or chef will come out
soon."

It took a few minutes, but eventually a

busboy exited the kitchen with a tray of glasses.

"Did I hear correctly that the keys are lost?"

He put the tray on the bar. "We're closed," he replied in a tone that expressed he was not in the mood for questions. "The Belmont Café is still serving lunch."

"Are you opening for dinner?" asked Dean.

"It's yet to be determined, but the Belmont —"

"We're looking for a friend," I interrupted. "There's a chance he might be locked in the food supply closet."

"That's ridiculous," said the man.

"Maybe," I replied. "But can we take a look?"

"No. Kitchen rules. Health code violations. Hotel rules. Need more?"

"Would you mind checking?" asked Dean. "Then we'll move on."

The man's gaze shifted to his hand. "Can't. The door is locked."

A crash came from the kitchen.

The man's eyes grew wide and he pushed through the swinging door. We followed him into the kitchen.

"Someone's in there," yelled a line cook as he pointed at the closed door. "I just

219

heard a noise."

"Either that or it's rats," said a waiter, who faltered when he saw us standing there. "Sorry, forget I said that." He glanced at the door. "But there's definitely something in there."

"Law enforcement, we need to get that door open," said Dean as he pulled the handle. It didn't budge. "How do we get in here?"

The waiter shrugged. "That's not our lock. Never been on there before."

I stared at the large padlock looped through the latch. "Can we get something to open this? Maybe a hammer or a crowbar?" I yelled to the rest of the kitchen. "Anyone?" I looked at Dean.

He had his phone out, ready to dial.

I put my ear to the door. A rocking noise came from inside. "I hear something and it could be a person." I stared at the staff. "And if they die because you didn't open it up, this is on your head."

"I'll do it," said the head chef as he grabbed a large meat cleaver. "I've been wanting to do this for the last twenty minutes anyway. We have a kitchen to run." He lifted the blade as I put my arms behind my back, knowing how easily it could take off one of my hands.

With two chops, the lock fell from the door. I rushed forward and opened it. There was Hudson, rocking back and forth on a chair at the far corner of the supply closet.

The kitchen staff gasped.

His mouth was gagged and ropes tied him to the chair.

I pulled the bandana away as I reached him. "Hudson, are you okay?"

Hudson lifted his head, blinked a few times, and dropped it again. "I will be."

I worked on the ropes, but they were tied knot over knot. "These aren't coming loose. I need a knife." I had my wine opener, but I knew the small blade on the end would take a long time to make any progress. "Can we get that knife back?" I yelled out to the kitchen.

"Here, I've got it." Dean leaned forward with a switchblade and cut through the rope on both sides.

"You carry a knife?" I asked.

Dean focused on Hudson. "Who did this?"

Hudson brought his wrists forward and tried to work on the remaining knots, which looped like bracelets, but his fingers stopped moving.

"Here, let me." Now that the tension was off the ropes, I was able to pull them apart.

"Thank you," breathed Hudson as he rubbed his wrists, both of them red.

"Who did this?" repeated Dean.

Hudson looked up at him, his eyes half closed from exhaustion. "I've missed seminars." He stood up and stumbled.

"Don't worry, people have been covering for you. Let's get you into the fresh air." I held Hudson's arm to steady him.

"Okay, I'm a little woozy on my feet. Nothing that some food and a glass of wine won't fix." He smiled weakly as the three of us walked out of the closet.

The head chef clapped and the rest of the staff waited for a moment before proceeding with their work for the day, retrieving items from the storage closet.

We reached the dining room and I pulled out a chair for Hudson. "Here, sit down. I'll find you a glass of water." I motioned to a waiter.

Dean took out his phone.

"What are you doing?" asked Hudson.

"Reporting this."

"Don't," he replied. "It's all a misunderstanding and I'm not pressing charges."

"Why not?" I asked.

"Doesn't matter." Hudson shook his head. "How long was I gone?"

"We don't know," I replied. "It depends

on when you were taken, but people have been looking for you since this morning."

Hudson rubbed the back of his neck. "What a weekend. Thanks for rescuing me. If you guys hadn't found me, I don't know how long I would have been in there."

A waiter brought a glass of water over to the table and set it down.

"Thank you," said Hudson, but he didn't reach for it. He rubbed his wrists again and looked at his watch. "Wow, it's that late? No wonder I'm starving. I think there's a dinner I have to get to." He stood up. "Hopefully I can come up with a good reason for missing the seminars."

"The authorities need to be notified of this," said Dean.

"No, they don't. Everything is fine now. If I don't want to press charges, there's nothing you can do, right?" He looked at both of us. "Thanks again for your help."

"Hudson, you can't be serious. You were kidnapped and tied up." I stared at him.

"I am serious. Katie Stillwell, promise me that you won't call the police." He was unflinching in his response.

I didn't move, but he seemed to take my lack of rebuttal as a positive.

He downed the glass of water and placed it on the table as he put on a rehearsed smile. "It's time to see the festival goers." He walked out of the restaurant, the door swinging as he went.

I stared after him. "What was that about?"

"I don't know," said Dean.

"Do you think he's faking it? Did he tie himself up?"

Dean shook his head. "The knots were tight and he couldn't have locked the door. Either someone actually tied him up, or he has a helper."

"But why would he do that?"

"I'm not sure, but I'm calling this in."

"Dean, he said he didn't want the police."

"Between this and your car incident this morning, I think someone is coming after both of you. It's better to be on the safe side and keep them updated."

I stared at the door, which was still swinging from Hudson's exit, while Dean made his call. How was being tied up in a closet a misunderstanding, and why didn't Hudson want the police involved? He was hiding something and I wanted to know what it was. I rushed to the entrance of the restaurant and looked into the hall. Hudson had already vanished.

TWENTY-SEVEN:
PAIRING SUGGESTION:
CABERNET FRANC —
BOURGUEIL, FRANCE

A red wine with high acidity that
pairs well with food and situations.

"The Standard room," replied Dean as he met me at the door, the folded festival booklet in his hand. "That's where the wine dinner is."

"How did you know that's where I was going?"

"Because, Katie Stillwell, I know you."

"Are the police coming?"

"Not at the moment, but they'll keep a close eye on Hudson. Come on." Dean grabbed my hand and we headed down the hall. When we reached the main lobby, we found Hudson in a heated discussion with Mr. Tinsley near one of the ballrooms.

"I'd fire you right now, Mr. Wiley, except I don't want the negative media attention. I've built this festival from the ground up and I won't let your shenanigans ruin it."

"I'm sorry, Mr. Tinsley. I don't know how many times I can say it, but this wasn't my fault."

"If he had reported it to the police," I whispered to Dean, "at least there would be some backup to his story."

"A likely excuse, Mr. Wiley. You've been nothing but trouble since the moment you arrived. I don't know how I can salvage this festival with only one day left." He straightened the clipboard in his hand. "You're lucky I can't express my full disappointment at the moment. I have to maintain some dignity — or what little is left after yet another disaster."

"Believe me, I was kidnapped and tied up. I wouldn't have missed the seminars otherwise."

"Really?" said Mr. Tinsley with a heavy tone of skepticism. "Who did this so-called injustice?"

Hudson paused. "I don't know." He glanced around and noticed us watching from the side. "There. They can back me up. Katie and Dean. They're the ones who found me."

Mr. Tinsley studied us. "Is this correct, Ms. Stillwell?"

I nodded but didn't step forward. I wanted to keep my distance for the time being. "He was locked in the food supply closet in the kitchen."

Mr. Tinsley put his hand to his head. "I guess that means police will be back here any minute. Wonderful. Another distraction," he said with exasperation.

"They're not coming," replied Dean.

Mr. Tinsley's eyebrows creased together.

"At the request of Mr. Wiley," he added.

Mr. Tinsley returned his attention to Hudson. "Well then, that's the first positive thing I've heard all day. No matter the reason, I don't like when drama comes into my festival. Are you someone who attracts drama, Mr. Wiley? We've worked together a long time but perhaps this is a new side I haven't seen."

"No, everything is fine. I will be at every single event the rest of the festival, even if it kills me."

I winced at Hudson's choice of words.

"We'll see," said Mr. Tinsley as he turned on his heels and walked away.

Hudson rubbed his forehead. "Thanks for helping me out there. I appreciate it."

"I can't understand your reasons for the delay," said Dean as he approached Hudson. "I think it's time you gave a statement to the police about the kidnapping."

"No, I need to focus on the festival. In

fact, everything is fine," said Hudson, a distant look on his face as he stared down the hall. "It's all going to be fine."

"Mr. Wiley," started Dean.

"No." He put his hand on the back of his neck and stretched. "It's okay."

"Wait," I said, wanting to take advantage of the moment with him. "When you mentioned Tama yesterday, did you mean the winery?"

He nodded.

"What's the connection? Why did you say it?"

"You don't know?"

"Perhaps you can enlighten us," added Dean.

"It's Jocelyn's company."

"Except her name wasn't Jocelyn," I said.

"The woman who was killed has been identified as Rachel Carlson," added Dean. "Sound familiar?"

Hudson continued to stare at us but didn't say anything. He looked at his watch and back at us. "I have to get to the dinner, but here," he said as he brought out two paper tickets from his pocket. "You can be my guests tonight."

"Did you know her name was Rachel?" I pressed.

"No, I didn't. But you both should come

228

to the dinner." Hudson pushed the tickets forward again. "Please."

I hesitated and took them.

"Katie," said Dean in a nervous tone as Hudson walked away.

"There's no way I'm missing that dinner. I want to find out what's going on." I looked at Dean. "Want to be my date?"

"To a suspicious dinner? Of course." Though his tone said differently. "But primarily because I refuse to leave your side." He stayed silent as we reached the Standard room and handed our tickets to the attendant.

Four tables with ten chairs each filled the room, with several people already sitting and more flowing in behind us.

Dean and I took seats at the table closest to the door. Two large shrimp on a bed of lettuce with a wedge of lemon had already been preset as the first course and a small menu above each plate denoted the upcoming dishes and the wines complementing each one. The fifth and final course included one of my favorite classic pairings: Stilton and Port. The sweetness of the Port paired perfectly with the tangy blue cheese.

"This looks like it's going to be a good dinner."

"I agree," said Dean, but his focus was on

Hudson, who stood at the front of the room. "It'll be interesting."

"I want to apologize for my absence at certain events this weekend," said Hudson to the group once everyone was seated. "I know I'm not the only reason you came to this festival, but if I was a reason, I do apologize. I've spoken with Mr. Tinsley." He motioned to the row of waiters standing to the side. "And we're providing everyone here with a glass of Champagne in addition to the preset wines."

The waiters walked along the rows, pouring the Champagne.

"I don't think that was Mr. Tinsley's idea," I whispered to Dean. "I have a feeling Hudson is paying for it out of his own pocket."

Dean nodded.

"I know it doesn't make up for my absences," continued Hudson with a heavy tone of fatigue, "but I hope it will help. For now, please enjoy the Champagne and our first course."

"His game face isn't hiding his stress."

"He was tied up all day," replied Dean.

"And then dismissed it as if it was nothing. I wonder if his attacker is here." I glanced around the room and noticed Anita sitting at one of the tables. I hadn't talked to her since the bellhop confirmed she lied about talking to Rachel that night.

"I'd also like to announce," said Hudson as he stood up once more, "that I'm excited to start on a new adventure. An opportunity has come up this weekend and I'm happy to share that I'm going to be working with Tama Winery."

I looked at Dean so fast, I nearly tweaked my neck. "That's Rachel's company. The one she wanted him to join."

He nodded. "And he was determined to stay out of it. I wonder what changed his mind."

Twenty-Eight:
Pairing Suggestion:
Cabernet Blend —
Columbia Valley,
Washington

Often referred to as a red blend or a
Bordeaux blend, these wines are well
balanced and notable.

After the last course was served, guests chatted in groups, but Anita was nearly on her
own after several people left her table.

"You know how Rachel waved to someone
at the bar that night? It was Anita," I said to
Dean as I motioned to her. "I talked to her
and she said that Rachel only said hi, but I
know she was lying."

"How so?"

"I've learned a lot about people over the
years while working at Trentino. I can tell
when people are on first dates, when they're
having an awkward family gathering, or
when it's friends meeting up after years
apart. I can tell without even hearing a
word. It's in their body language. So I did a
little investigating and the bellhop said they

not only talked, they also left the lobby together. I think it's time I called her on it. Do you want to come?"

Dean glanced at the last bite of Stilton tart on his plate and then at Hudson. "No, I'll stay here and keep an eye on him. Be safe."

"I promise I won't leave the room without you."

"You better not."

I squeezed Dean's shoulder in reassurance as I stood up and approached her table. "Anita?"

She looked up from her phone. "Yes?"

"Remember, we met the other day."

"That's right! We're old friends." She grinned.

"Mind if I sit?" I motioned to the empty chairs.

"Sure thing, but isn't the dinner over?"

"It is, but I just want to chat for a second." I sat down. "Did you enjoy the dinner?"

"I did. What great dishes! And I love all that wine. It's fun, isn't it?"

"It is." I debated on how to proceed. "Listen, since you and I are old friends, can we be honest with each other?"

Anita stared at me but didn't visually or verbally respond.

"It's nothing bad," I added.

"Okay," she replied slowly. "I just feel like you're about to drop a bomb on me and I haven't had enough wine for that."

I glanced at the five glasses on the table in front of her from the pairings. All of them were empty. "I'd like to know more about Jocelyn Rivers."

"Who's that?"

"The attendee who died. The one you waved to." I didn't want to say her real name was Rachel. Not yet.

"Oh, that's right. That poor girl." Anita picked up a wineglass and shook the remaining drops into her mouth.

"So here comes the moment I need you to be honest with me. You only met her at the opening ceremonies, right?"

"That's right." She moved her bangs out of her eyes.

"Are you sure about that?"

"What do you mean?"

"I have a feeling there's more to that story," I remarked. "When Jocelyn waved to you from the bar that night, she said that you were an old friend. I think you guys said more than just a quick hi." I took a breath as I decided to put all of my cards on the table. "There's a witness who said you talked for a bit, and I'd like to hear the truth from you instead of the police. They're

234

already involved and I'm going to have to tell them you know more." It was a risk saying it, but it was almost a relief as I did.

"There's definitely not enough wine here," Anita replied as she picked up another empty glass and set it down. "But fine, so here's the deal. I only met her on Thursday. That part's true. But I may have fibbed a little when you asked me earlier."

"Why? And which part?"

"Because you said she died and you had seen her wave at me. It scared me. Maybe you thought I knew something. Why would I give you more reason to think that?" Anita shook her head. "You can't blame me for that. That's just human nature."

Several guests were leaving the room and I knew my time was running out to ask Anita more questions.

"Totally valid," I replied. "So what part did you fib about?"

"If I tell you, does this mean I have to talk to the police?"

Dean had finished his tart and was pretending to look at his phone, but I could tell he was watching Hudson. "I'm not sure. What was it?"

"Okay, it's not a big deal, but she paid me a hundred dollars to make sure she talked to Hudson Wiley." Anita shrugged. "It had nothing to do with her death."

"How do you know it had nothing to do with it?"

"Because it was all over and done with before she died. The reason she waved to me in the bar was because she'd reached her goal. She was sitting with Hudson, so I didn't need to do any more after that."

"What would you have done?"

"I was going to be her wingman, of sorts. Start talking to Hudson and then she could come up and join us. That's all."

"Why would she pay you one hundred dollars for that?"

"She saw me talking to him at the opening ceremonies and figured I knew him. She asked if I was looking to make a quick buck." Anita laughed. "At first I thought she was hitting on me. Jocelyn was pretty, but not my type." She took lipstick out of her purse and applied it. "But I decided to help her because a little extra money never hurt." She shrugged. "We all have our secret agendas or conquests, if that's what Hudson was for her. But I let each person do their own thing, you know? It's better that way."

I nodded. "Since you didn't exactly do what she wanted, I guess you didn't get paid."

"Oh, I got paid. Right after the wave. She

was so happy that she was with him in the bar and apparently she was getting a lot of money to talk to him. She wanted to pass along the 'joy' she called it." Anita looked at the nearby empty tables. "We should go. I don't want to be the last ones."

I glanced around the room. There were only four people left, including Hudson and Dean. "Who was paying her?"

She looked at me, her green eyes strong and focused. "I'm telling you the truth this time. I really don't know."

I processed the information. "She waved to you, came up to you in the lobby, and paid you right as I was watching." Though I didn't see it happen. At the time, I was focused on the blind tasting.

"Actually, it was kind of funny because she ushered me into the ladies' room, like it was all clandestine and stuff. I don't know why she didn't want anyone to see us. The money transfer was quick and it's not like the lobby was full of people. But I guess everyone has their reasons. Maybe she didn't want people to see me with the money, in case I got mugged or something." Anita thought for a moment. "Actually, that was rather sweet of her."

"In the bathroom? Did she have anyone waiting in there?"

Anita laughed. "It was the ladies' room. Who would she have with her? She said thanks and she handed me a hundred-dollar bill. I tried to push it back. Frankly, I felt guilty for taking that money. Like I said, I didn't do anything. But she insisted, so I put it in my purse, thanked her, and went on my way."

"Where's the money now?"

Anita studied me. "Why? It's mine. I don't care what kind of investigation you're doing, you don't get the money."

"No, sorry, that's not what I meant. I just —" I hesitated, unsure of how to say my next part. "I just had an idea in case it was counterfeit. I mean, it was rather generous of her to give you the money."

"I don't think it was counterfeit. I've already spent it. I paid my bar tab with it and the bartender held it up to the light and checked for that string thing."

I nodded. It was weird how Rachel insisted on paying Anita. Either she was a genuine person who followed through on her promises or she was trying to cover all of her tracks. "Did you know her name wasn't Jocelyn?"

"It wasn't? What was it?"

"Rachel."

"Get out. Like she was on a secret mission or something?" Anita picked up her purse. "Well, this was fun, but I should get going." She stood up and then sat back down. "Actually, I just remembered something."

My heart rate accelerated. "What?"

"It might be nothing, but she had a bottle of wine with her. I didn't think anything of it at first. I mean, it's a wine festival, right? But she took the bottle out of her purse, laughed, and said someone would be seriously ticked if they knew she was going to drink it. I figured she had taken it from the bar. I didn't care much. I just wanted to get my money and get out of there."

"Do you know who she thought would be ticked?"

"Maybe the person paying her? I don't know. That really is all I can tell you." She stood up.

I closed my eyes and went back to the scene of Rachel's death. I focused in on the bottle in her hand. "Did the wine have purple writing on it?"

She thought for a moment. "Yeah. Purple writing and shapes on the label."

I had seen it recently, at Walt and Ben's table in the bar. Tama Winery, the same one that Hudson just announced a partnership with. At least now I knew exactly why Rachel had tried to get into the festival and why she was so eager to get to Hudson. Someone had paid her to push Tama wine on him. But who?

"It's time for me to go. I have a feeling the bars are going to be rocking tonight. I might try the Lancaster. I've heard good things."

"Thanks again for your help."

"You got it, old friend." Anita winked and left the room.

I looked around, but Dean's seat was empty and Hudson was gone, too. I was alone.

I found Dean in the hallway, leaning against the wall as he stared at the far end by the lobby.

"Everything okay?"

"Keeping an eye on Hudson," said Dean. "He went that way with a group of people, but I didn't want to leave you." He looked at me. "How's Anita?"

"She's fine, but this whole thing revolves around Tama Winery." An idea went through my head like wine flowing from a decanter into a glass, splashing up the sides. "Listen, I need to find the bottle of wine that Rachel had."

"I'm not following."

"The one that was in her hand."

240

"It's evidence and part of an active murder investigation. They won't release it and I'm not going to get it out of evidence for you, even if I could," said Dean.

"No, I wouldn't ask you to do that." I stared at the empty hallway as I thought about where I could go. "I just need to find another one."

"Why?" asked Dean.

I looked at him. "To trap the killer."

Twenty-Nine:
Pairing Suggestion:
Pinot Noir —
Central Otago,
New Zealand

A similar style to California Pinot Noir
but with more spice.

I walked down the hall at such a fast speed, Dean could barely keep up.

"Where are we going?"

"To the bar. I want to find out if they have the wine."

"Which one?"

"Tama Winery, the one that Hudson announced tonight. Walt and Ben had a bottle and it wasn't from the Lancaster, so I'm hoping it was from here."

We arrived in the New Sierra bar. There were a few people seated at the tables but Hudson was not one of them.

"Welcome back," said the bartender. He was the same one from when I had a drink with Isabella. "What can I get you?"

"Actually, can I see your wine list?"

He handed over the folder and attended

to other customers.

I scanned it, but Tama wasn't on the list. "Nope, no Tama."

"Walt and Ben are walking through the lobby. You said they had a bottle, correct?"

"Yes, but they wouldn't say where they got it. They only said it was from a friend." I stared at Walt and Ben. They noticed and headed in our direction.

"A friend who kills?" asked Dean.

"Possibly."

"Don't I know you from somewhere?" said Ben as they stopped a few feet away. "Oh, that's right. You're the one who schooled Walt in the blind tasting." He smiled.

"Thanks for bringing it back up," said Walt.

"My pleasure," replied Ben.

"Coming here for a drink?"

"Nope," said Walt as he flipped a cork in the air. "We're on a mission."

I glanced at Dean and back at them. Could their mission be the same one we were on? "Care to share your flight plan?"

"Walt here has a hankering for a certain whiskey and apparently they have it at the other hotel." He motioned toward the Lancaster.

"They do," replied Walt. "I saw it there

yesterday. And if you say *apparently* again, I'm going to make you buy it for me, because it actually exists. Nothing apparent about it."

Ben stayed silent, though it was clear he was biting his tongue.

"Didn't want to stay with wine, the theme of the weekend?" I smiled.

"Call it palate fatigue," said Walt. "Or perhaps just a craving for a single malt Scotch."

"Not another bottle of Tama?" I added.

Walt gave a side glance to Ben. "Not tonight, maybe tomorrow."

"Want to join us?" asked Ben.

"Not at the moment," said Dean.

"Come by when you can," said Walt as he turned his attention to me. "Unless it's like yesterday, where you pull out mad skills and can tell us what the whiskey is just by tasting it."

"I like whiskey, but no more blind tasting. At least not tonight."

"What about you, Dean? How are you with the non-wine drinks?"

Dean smiled. "While I do love a good Scotch, particularly the smoky and peaty styles of Islay, and I enjoy the grassy styles of Speyside, I've been known to stick to a good old Kentucky Bourbon."

I stared at Dean. All of this was news to me.

"Nice," said Ben.

"Perhaps we'll join you later," Dean continued.

"You got it, chief," said Walt who seemed clearly impressed by Dean's knowledge. The two of them walked away.

"Okay, wait a minute. How did I not know you knew all of this about whiskey and Scotch?"

Dean shrugged as a tinge of pink filled his cheeks. "You love wine so I enjoy talking about wine with you."

"But you never mentioned it?"

"I like to talk about what's important to you."

"Yes, but we need to share more. And you and I are going to drink some whiskey soon." Although wine was my passion and career, I also loved exploring whiskey, beer, sake, and other liquors. Every bottle had a story to tell.

Dean motioned to the nearby bar table. "Let's take a seat."

"Detective Stillwell, where's your investigative spirit? I thought you would be more interested in solving this than having a drink."

Dean stifled a laugh. "Standing here isn't

going to do any good except call attention to ourselves. I suggest we sit, talk it over, and figure out our next step. Together. Unless I'm not allowed to help."

"I'd love your help. We make a great team." I pulled out the chair at a corner table and sat down. Several of the tables were occupied, but we still had our privacy.

"So there's no Tama wine here," said Dean. "What next?"

"I'm not sure yet, but I need a bottle of it to make this work," I replied. "It's the key element to the crime."

"Considering Hudson just announced his partnership with Tama, he might have a bottle, but I have a feeling that won't work for your plan."

"No, it won't."

Dean's face turned serious. "Do you think Hudson killed Rachel?"

"Even if he did, he had help. He couldn't tie himself up, you said that yourself. But afterward, he changed his tune about representing the winery."

"Katie, I don't think just locking him in the closet would create that change."

"Neither do I." I stared into Dean's eyes. "Blackmail."

"What would they be blackmailing him about?"

"I don't know. Maybe he did something not so great in the past." I put my hand up. "But listen, Anita said someone paid Rachel to push Tama on Hudson. So either she was killed because she didn't do that, or because she didn't take Hudson to whomever she was supposed to that night. He said she wanted him to meet someone."

"We don't know who that was."

"No, but there's a way we can find out."

"Katie, be careful."

"Why do you say that?"

"Because your ideas often involve some amount of danger."

"There's nothing dangerous with what I'm about to do. I've used my deductive wine skills to solve other murders, right? But what if this time, I make the other person use theirs?"

"I'm not following."

"The killer was trying to get Hudson to endorse the wine, right? That's who paid Rachel. And when you work with a certain wine a lot, you know every nuance, every subtle characteristic within it. Tama Winery isn't well known, at least not yet. If someone tonight identifies the taste of Tama wine, then we know they're involved with the winery and possibly behind this whole thing with Hudson and Rachel."

"What about Walt and Ben? They had the wine last night. They might recognize it."

"I don't know if tasting one bottle would be enough for them to identify it. Also, maybe they're involved."

Dean shook his head. "Even if you hide the label at first, they're going to see it eventually and know it's Tama."

I stared across the room. "Unless it's not in a Tama bottle."

"Katie, what are you up to?"

"I'm going to pour it into a different wine bottle. If someone still recognizes it as theirs, then we know they're involved." I put my hands out and shrugged as I made an innocent face. "Just doing a little transferring of wine. Nothing dangerous about it."

He shook his head as a slight grin appeared. "You never cease to amaze me, Katie Stillwell."

"I hope it's always that way. We need to get together everyone who has a connection to Tama and I need one of their wines to make it all work."

"How will you do that? They don't sell it here."

"I don't know. This is where I'm stuck." I outlined a scratch on the tabletop with my finger. "Even if we drive up to the winery, which is about an hour away, they wouldn't be open right now."

"Maybe a local wine shop has it? I'll make some calls."

"You will?"

"I want to help, but know that I'm only doing this because I care for you. I know how you get yourself into situations and since I'm here, the best thing I can do is keep you out of danger." He took out his phone.

"Thanks, I really appreciate it." I glanced around at the tables. If I was going to trap the killer, the bar here at the New Sierra would be the best place. Walt, Ben, and Hudson had spent most of their evenings over at the Lancaster bar. They would know that wine list too well. "Be right back."

I returned to the bartender and glanced at his name badge before speaking. "Tom, I'm going to come in here with some friends soon, hopefully in the next hour. Can I reserve that side table?" I pointed to a larger one with nine seats ready to accommodate a group.

He glanced at the table. "It's first come, first serve," he replied. "We don't do reservations."

I sighed. "Okay, can we pretend that I'm already sitting there now and have just stood up for a moment? Which would actually be longer, but I digress." I put a twenty on the bar. "This can be my first drink. Maybe I'm going to spend the next hour drinking it."

Tom smiled as he picked up the twenty. He pulled a folded RESERVED sign from behind the bar. "Here, go claim your table."

"Thank you. One last request. Can I buy an empty bottle of red wine from you?"

"You're joking."

"No, I'm really not." I stared at him while I waited for a response. "I want to pay for the bottle in full, but I want it to be empty."

"I've had some strange requests in my time, but this one is throwing me for a loop. Is this so you can sit at the table and not order drinks?"

"Don't worry, we're ordering drinks tonight. I just need to show a bottle to some of my friends. It's part of a blind tasting trick."

Tom studied me for a moment and then reached below the counter. I heard the clanking of bottles. He poured the last few drops from a bottle of Rubywood Cabernet into a glass. "Here, this one was about to go into the recycling bin anyway. It's all yours."

I took the bottle and turned it label side down in the crook of my arm to hide the name. "Perfect. Thank you. I'll see you in a bit."

"Sure," said Tom, clearly puzzled by my actions.

I was set. Now to find each of the players.

Thirty:
Pairing Suggestion:
Malbec — Cahors, France

This region produces Malbec, also called Cot, with firm tannins and structure.

Dean put down his phone as I returned to the table. "You're pretty lucky."

"To have you? I definitely am."

Dean smiled. "Well, yes, but there's a bottle of Tama Cabernet in Solvang."

"Perfect. The empty bottle is a Cab, too. That works great."

"Except they close in thirty minutes."

I stared at Dean. "Okay, how about this. Can you go get it while I get everyone gathered here?"

"No. A car tried to hit you and Hudson was tied up. I'm not leaving your side."

"If we both go, we may lose the opportunity to get everyone together. This wine is the only way to figure out what's going on. What if I can prevent something worse happening?" I put my hand on his. "I promise I'll be careful and I'll be waiting here when you return."

"Why does this go against all of my instincts?"

"You can't protect me at every turn. I'll be fine. Come on, the shop is closing soon. We'll walk over to the Lancaster together. I need to grab a bag for this." I lifted my arm with the Rubywood nestled in my elbow. "Then I'll talk to Walt and Ben there."

Dean was silent as we exited the hotel.

A few people strolled about on the lawn, but other than that, the night was quiet.

"I still don't like this."

"I promise I'll be in the New Sierra bar when you get back. Besides, I've fought off killers before." I smiled, but it was lost on Dean. I returned to my serious tone. "I'll be safe."

We reached the Lancaster.

Dean stared into my eyes. "Keep on your guard, try not to be alone, and I'll be back as soon as I can."

"I'll be careful. I'll see you at the New Sierra."

He kissed me and headed to the parking lot.

I kept my head down in the lobby of the Lancaster, not wanting anyone to see me with the bottle. I made it to my room and put the bottle in a large bag, a feeling of relief washing over me. My plan was in motion. Now I needed to find everyone who could be connected with Tama Winery or Rachel Carlson.

I returned to the lobby and saw Anita in the bar with Walt and Ben, three of the people I needed to find. But the sight of them sitting at the same table shocked me. Were they all in this together?

"Rick, Roll, Anita," I said as I arrived at their table. "How do you three know each other?"

"Just met them today," said Anita. "They're so fun."

"Katie's pouring at tomorrow's event. She's going to pour a little heavy for us," added Walt.

"Good to know," remarked Anita. "You're my new favorite wine snob."

I stiffened at the reference but faked a smile. "Hey, so do you want to join me for drinks in the bar over at the New Sierra in a few minutes?"

"What about drinks here? Chair. Bar." Walt pointed to each item as he said them. "Drinks." He smiled. "It's like a math equation and I just solved it for you. You're welcome."

"That's great, but I'm going to open up a

special bottle over there. You might not want to miss it. That's all I'm saying."

"Why don't you open it here?" asked Ben. "There's plenty of chairs available at our fingertips." He touched the empty seat next to him. "See," he added.

"I already have a table reserved," I said. "Be there, or don't, but don't say I didn't offer you the opportunity." Walt and Ben locked eyes and I knew they would be there. "So I'll see you guys in a few?"

"I don't know," said Anita.

"What?" Her statement surprised me.

"I'm just kidding, you fool. Of course I want to try this special bottle." She laughed and put up her hands. " 'Special bottle,' " she repeated with air quotes. "We'll come over after we finish this round."

"Great," I replied. "See you in a bit."

I left the Lancaster and headed back to the New Sierra, the lack of light on the lawn sending a shiver through me. I didn't like the dark and, with the car episode earlier, I knew someone was after me and this was a perfect opportunity to follow through. I quickened my pace and was relieved when I entered the brightly lit lobby. Hudson was standing with two people I didn't know at the far end, and nearby, Isabella was talking to Mr. Tinsley.

"Ms. Stillwell," said Mr. Tinsley. "I trust you're having a good evening."

"I am. In fact, I'm just about to meet some friends at the bar for a drink. Would you both like to join me?" I glanced at each of them. Isabella looked as timid as ever.

"I'm afraid I can't," said Mr. Tinsley. "The way this festival has been going, I find I need to keep a literal thumb on every detail." He held up his hand to show the smudged pen marks on his thumb.

"Understood." I turned to Isabella. "What about you?"

She glanced around. "Um, sure. That would be nice."

"What are we all talking about here?" asked Hudson as he joined the group.

"I invited Isabella and Mr. Tinsley to join me for drinks at the bar. I have Walt, Ben, and Anita coming, too. I'm going to open up a special wine."

"One from here?"

"Not exactly," I replied. "It's a unique one and I think you'll be pleased. It would be a shame to miss it."

Hudson studied me for a moment. "I'll be there. When?"

I glanced at my watch, though it was just a delay tactic. "About ten minutes."

"That's ideal," said Mr. Tinsley. "Mr.

Wiley, you and I can speak about some of tomorrow's activities first."

"I'll see you all in a few. And Mr. Tinsley, if you change your mind, there'll be a seat there for you."

"My appearance is unlikely as this point, but thank you for the offer."

I looked at Isabella to see if she wanted to accompany me to the table, but she seemed like she was waiting to talk to Hudson. I headed toward the bar to wait for everyone to arrive.

Hopefully Dean returned with the wine before they did.

THIRTY-ONE:
PAIRING SUGGESTION:
SUPER TUSCAN —
TUSCANY, ITALY

A red wine made with grapes
not indigenous to Italy, such as Merlot,
Syrah, and Cabernet Sauvignon.

Walt, Ben, and Anita strolled in a few minutes later.

"You made it," I said as they sat down.

"You told us it was a special bottle. That was enough," said Ben. "Where is it?"

"It's coming. The night is young," I replied.

"Well, I'm not. I feel like I'm aging by the minute," said Anita. She waved her hand at the waiter. "I'll have a glass of the Chardonnay."

"Me, too," said Ben. "Only, not Chardonnay. What does Ben want? Zin. Yes, Zin."

"Zin here, too," said Walt.

Isabella pulled out a chair and sat down. "Am I late?"

I looked at her. "Not at all."

"The wine isn't even here," said Ben.

"Is Hudson coming?" asked Isabella in her usual nervous tone.

"I thought you were with him?"

"No, he was still with Mr. Tinsley the last I saw him." She glanced around and I did, too.

There was still no sign of Dean. The empty bottle of Rubywood was waiting in my bag, but I thought I would have the real wine before everyone convened. Now it was too late.

The waiter placed the three glasses on the table.

"Okay, I'm here, the party can start," said Hudson as he took a seat. "What's everyone drinking?"

"Chardonnay," said Anita. "But apparently Katie is holding us in suspense over some special bottle."

"That's right," said Hudson. "Where is the wine of the hour?"

"Who knows," replied Walt. "Left all sorts of fun whiskey drinks back at the Lancaster only to sit here and wait."

"They were empty," said Ben.

"I could have ordered more," said Walt.

"Katie." Dean's voice came from behind me along with a wave of relief. "Can I talk to you for a moment?"

"Ooh, someone's in trouble," said Anita. Ben and Walt laughed.

"Excuse me, I'll be right back." I followed Dean into the lobby.

He pulled a wine bottle wrapped in a plastic bag out of his coat. "It wasn't easy. The store was closing when I pulled up."

"Thanks." I glanced inside the bag. The purple writing on the Tama bottle was the same as I had seen before. Now it was time to make this work. "I have to do a little decanting. Can you keep the group occupied? I don't want them to get restless and leave."

"On it."

Dean headed to the table while I put the bottle of Tama next to the empty one in my bag and walked toward the women's restroom. I acted like I was going there for a normal reason, but I still felt I looked suspicious.

The restroom's marble floor and countertop were impeccably clean and all four stalls were open. At least I had the place to myself to proceed with my plan. I had decanted expensive bottles, careful not to let the sediment leave the bottle with the wine, but I had never poured wine into another bottle. This was going to be a very different experience than I was used to.

I set my bag on the counter and took out the empty Rubywood, but the door caught my attention. If someone came in, such as Isabella or Anita, I would be caught red-handed. I needed to be more discreet. I glanced around.

The stall.

The idea of pouring wine in there was ridiculous, but I knew it was the safest bet.

I went in and placed my bag on the hook as I closed the door. My wine opener easily removed the cork on the Tama bottle and I put it in my pocket along with the foil from the top.

There was a slight tremor to my right hand as I held both bottles so I took a deep breath, but my tight lungs wouldn't expand. I didn't know how long Dean could keep them occupied at the table so I wouldn't have a chance to calm myself. It was time to pour.

Bottle to bottle was a whole different skill from my usual routine, yet the wine flowed into the opening in a small stream. Maybe this could be an addition to the Advanced Exam that already included decanting.

The bathroom door opened.

My lungs seized but I kept pouring, knowing that if I stopped, there was a chance drips could mar the label and the game would be over.

Heels clicked across the bathroom floor, pausing briefly in front of my stall before entering the next one. Would she wonder if something was wrong if I stayed quiet for a long time? I didn't know who it was, but there was a chance it could be Isabella or Anita. Dean might have said I stepped away to the ladies' room. If she asked me what was going on, I would be stuck.

My hand wavered and a splash of red wine missed the opening.

Two drops crawled down the neck. I stopped pouring, but I didn't have a free hand to wipe the wine away and there wasn't time to put down a bottle.

The drops continued toward the Ruby-wood label and then diverted to the side, missing the paper entirely. I breathed out with relief.

I held off on pouring until the lady was washing her hands.

The rest of the wine was soon in the new bottle and I pushed in the cork to complete the ploy. It was show time.

I put both bottles in my bag and washed my hands at the sink. A woman walked into the restroom and I smiled at her, thinking, *Yep, just washing my hands. Totally didn't just pour wine from one bottle to another while standing in the stall.*

I returned to the table where the six of them still waited. Dean had done a good job of keeping everyone there.

"Everything okay?" asked Dean as I sat down.

"Yes, sorry. Just needed a little extra time."

"Are we going to try this special bottle, or did you just get us over here so we could ask your boyfriend lots of questions while you were gone?" remarked Anita.

Dean's face was stoic, but I could tell there was a little unease.

"Ah, it wasn't that bad," said Hudson. "Dean was a good sport about it. But how about this wine you mentioned?"

"Yes." I kept the Rubywood bottle in the bag under the table as I opened it, not wanting to reveal that the foil had already been cut off. "Coming right up."

"It's about time," said Anita.

"The anticipation was forcing me to drink," replied Walt.

"Me, too," added Ben.

I motioned to the waiter. "Can I get six glasses?"

The waiter looked at the bottle I hid with my hands under the table. "Sorry, but we don't allow outside wine in here."

"Can you check with Tom? I cleared it

with him earlier."

The waiter hesitated and walked to the bar. Tom glanced over and gave me a thumbs up. The waiter returned with six empty glasses.

"Why only six? There are seven of us." Isabella glanced around at the group.

"I'm not drinking," said Dean.

"This is a group activity," said Walt. "We all need to participate."

"One of us should stay sober," replied Dean. "It's been an interesting weekend."

I kept the label away from everyone as I poured a few ounces into each glass.

"So sommelier Katie Stillwell," said Hudson. "Are you going to tell us about this wine as you serve it?"

"Not quite yet. I'm going to wait for you to try it first."

"Can we know where it's from?" asked Ben.

"From a friend," I replied with a smile. "But I can't wait to hear what you think." I finished pouring the last glass and sat back.

Anita picked hers up and took a sip. "Nice but not one that I would say was worth all the fuss." She looked at me. "Sorry. I didn't mean to say that. I just mean that we've tried a lot of great wine this weekend."

"It's fine," I replied.

Ben and Walt tasted their glasses and shrugged.

"Not bad," said Ben. "Wait, is this like a blind taste test?" He tried it again. "Yep, this is a mysterious red wine from the collection of Katie Stillwell. What do I win?"

"Self satisfaction," I replied. They'd both had Tama wine the night before, but neither of them seemed to recognize it, especially as they had Merlot and this one was Cabernet. I had one last chance to show the fake name to see if anyone reacted. "Shall I do the reveal?"

"Please," replied Hudson.

"I'm on the edge of my seat," said Walt without any enthusiasm.

I held up the bottle of Rubywood Cabernet.

"You know, I think I've tried that before," said Hudson.

"Maybe not as special as you hoped it would be then," added Ben.

"He's a Master Sommelier. He's tried a lot of wine. But I thought it would be fun for the group."

Anita relaxed in her chair and Walt seemed distracted by people walking past in the lobby, while Ben drank more wine. No one seemed to know that it was Tama.

A wave of unease began in my chest as

my lungs tightened. Perhaps I had been wrong all along. Perhaps this wasn't the way to trap the killer.

Hudson put his glass down. "Let's order some new drinks. Full glasses this time. Anyone want to do a blind tasting? Katie?"

I shook my head.

"I might. I think I can do it now," said Ben as Walt laughed. "Oh, you laugh now, just you wait. Let's get some more wine."

"Here," said Walt as he held up the glass. "Tell us what wine this is."

"It's a . . ." Ben paused as he looked over at the Rubywood. "It's too far away and I don't have my glasses."

"I've never seen you wear glasses a day in your life. Wine goggles, maybe."

"May I see the bottle?" asked Isabella.

I handed it across the table.

She stared at the label and tasted the wine again.

I watched her closely. "Do you like it?"

"Oh," she replied as she realized I was staring at her. "It's nice." She smiled.

I nodded but continued to watch her. She took another sip from her glass.

"Is it okay?" I asked.

She jumped a little, in typical Isabella form. "Oh yes. It's just not what I was expecting from this winery."

"What were you expecting?"

She gave a nervous laugh. "I don't know. It just tastes like . . . Never mind." She put the bottle down but continued to stare at the label as she drank more of the wine. The look of confusion grew on her face.

I met eyes with Dean and gave a slight nod.

It was Isabella.

THIRTY-TWO:
PAIRING SUGGESTION:
SYRAH —
WALLA WALLA, WASHINGTON

An excellent region for Syrah,
these wines are made from grapes
with thick skins.

After Walt and Ben cabbed it to their house and Isabella and Anita headed upstairs at the New Sierra, I pulled Dean aside in the lobby.

"No one else seemed to think anything about the wine, but Isabella knew it was Tama. She has to be the one who paid Rachel to get to Hudson."

"Katie, just because she knew the wine doesn't mean she killed Rachel."

"No, it doesn't. We need more proof." I glanced at the bar, where Hudson was having a drink with some more guests. "I wonder if he's still in danger."

"Hudson already announced that he's working with Tama. Isabella — if it is her — already accomplished her mission."

"Then why is she still here?"

"A lot of perpetrators want to watch the fallout from their actions," replied Dean.

Hudson stood up from his table in the bar, shook hands with the guests, and crossed the lobby, leaving the hotel through the side door.

I moved forward but felt Dean's hand on my arm.

"Katie, this is dangerous."

"I just want to make sure he gets to his room safely. I don't think the festival needs him missing again." It was partly the truth. I didn't like leaving Isabella in the hotel, knowing that she might be a killer, but I knew there was nothing else we could do at the moment.

Dean studied me. "Okay then."

We walked across the lawn toward the Lancaster. Hudson reached the front door and disappeared inside. I quickened my pace, Dean's speed matching mine. Hudson was still in the lobby when we stepped inside.

"At least he's here now and Isabella is staying at the other hotel. I just wish we had something more concrete."

"Let the police handle it. They'll find out," said Dean.

"I hope so."

"Mr. Dean Stillwell," said a loud voice from the front desk.

"The name game continues," I replied. "Sorry about that."

"I'm almost used to it by now," said Dean.

The attendant waved us over. "There's a message for you," he continued.

"I'm going to make sure Hudson gets in his room. I'll meet you upstairs in a few?"

Dean hesitated.

"We're in this hotel. Isabella is at the other one. And I'm only going upstairs."

Hudson stood near the elevator but the doors had opened.

"I'll be right there," said Dean. "Be safe."

I rushed over and Hudson held the elevator door for me. I stepped inside, hoping he wouldn't notice that I didn't push level two. "Ready for the last day tomorrow?"

"You have no idea," said Hudson as he rubbed his forehead.

"Great that the festival brought you new business. I mean, with Tama."

"Oh," he replied as he shifted uncomfortably. "Yeah. One more announcement to make about that at the grand tasting." He almost looked sad as he said it.

"I thought you didn't want to work with them. I mean, at least what you said Friday morning, about Jocelyn — I mean Rachel

270

— wanting your name on the business."

"No, it's all good now. It's all fine."

"So you're happy?" I asked, hoping he would drop some clues.

He faked a smile. "We'll talk about it tomorrow."

The doors opened to the third floor. Hudson walked to the right and I turned to the left so he wouldn't think I was following him.

"Night," I said as I glanced back over my shoulder.

"Night," he replied. Once the door to 303 was closed and he was safely in his room, I took the stairs down to the second floor.

The area was quiet, but that was to be expected. Most people were asleep.

I reached the end of the hallway where it turned to my room, but the overhead light was out.

An unease began in my chest. I didn't like the dark and the thought of what, or who, could be lurking.

A dim glow cast from the adjoining hallway, but it was the darkest near my room ten doors down. Great.

I thought about waiting for Dean or even going downstairs to meet him, but it was just a hallway bulb that had gone out. That was all. I would call the front desk and let them know and it would be fixed by morning. Everything would be fine.

I took out my phone and used the flashlight app. Although the beam of light was small, it did what it needed to do. I continued forward, glad I was finally in the habit of carrying my phone with me.

I held my room key. The antique charm of the hotel also meant they used actual keys instead of keycards.

I barely made it to the lock when two gloved hands slipped around my neck. They squeezed, taking my breath with them. I pulled at the arms of my attacker as my phone fell to the floor, the light illuminating the doorframe.

"I know what you're up to," said a gravelly voice as the grip tightened. I wasn't sure if the disguised voice was male or female, but my strength was no match against theirs. I clawed at the hands but the gloves made my efforts unsuccessful.

I needed air.

"If you mess this up for me," they continued, "I swear I'll kill you." The hands pushed me down as they released and I fell to the floor, gasping for breath. I glanced up, only to see the end of a dark coat rounding the lit corner.

I scrambled to grab the key from the floor.

My fingers located the cold metal and I jammed it into the lock, pushing the door open and slamming it behind me. I took huge gulps of air as I tried to catch my breath before I moved into the bathroom to look at my neck. The results of the attack were bright red lines that would most definitely turn into bruises by morning.

The door to the room opened and I jumped back, my hands up in fighting position.

"Katie?" asked Dean. "Your phone was in the hallway." He noticed my stance. "What's going on?"

I glanced in the mirror again, my adrenaline level lowering along with my fists. "See these?" I pointed to the marks.

"What happened?" Dean rushed over.

"Someone attacked me," I replied. "In the hallway just now. Tried to choke me." I rubbed my skin. "I'm fine," I quickly added. "But it was another warning."

Dean looked at my neck. "Are you okay?"

"Yes, I'm fine."

"We should get you checked out to make sure there's no serious injuries."

"Dean, I'm fine." I stared into his eyes. "Honest. I would tell you if I wasn't."

He nodded but his face was still strained with concern. "I didn't see anyone when I came up. Did you notice any identifying characteristics?"

"No," I said as I took a deep breath. "But I think it was Isabella. She warned me not to mess things up for her. Hudson's making another announcement about Tama tomorrow." I looked in the mirror. "I just had no idea she was this strong. Those long sleeves she wears must hide serious muscles. Maybe I need to start cross training instead of just running." I lifted my arm up in a faux flex.

"Not funny," said Dean.

"I agree. But it definitely gives me something to work on." I paused. "Maybe that's how she knew Rachel. She worked out at her fitness center." I looked at Dean. "What was the message at the front desk about anyway?"

"Nothing. A note about a schedule change on the Pinot Noir seminar."

"The one that happened yesterday? Nice. So they wanted to get you away from me. As if I couldn't fight them on my own."

Dean took out his phone. "I'm calling the police. This has gone too far."

"But Hudson still won't talk to them."

"No, but I need to keep you safe."

"And we don't have proof that Isabella did anything wrong. Even tonight. They'll interview her, she'll deny everything, and get away."

"But it'll be up to the local authorities. I'll tell them what we know and they'll take it from there." Dean looked at me with a softness in his eyes. "I don't think you should be at the festival tomorrow. We'll drive back early in the morning. You're being threatened. I can't have something happen to you."

"I have a responsibility to pour at the event and I feel fine. It was just a warning. No permanent damage." I put my hands on my hips. "Besides, I wasn't raised as a cop's daughter to shy away from a threat like that. They want to find me? Come and get me."

"Katie," Dean sighed. "I adore you, but sometimes you're a little stubborn."

"You could just say I'm focused."

"Okay, you're focused. Very focused. But I'm serious, you need to be careful tomorrow."

"I'm always careful."

"Yes, but I know you, and you also have a habit of getting yourself into trouble."

I smiled and pretended to shine the imaginary halo around my head. "I'll just be pouring at the event."

THIRTY-THREE:
PAIRING SUGGESTION:
BANDOL — PROVENCE, FRANCE

A Mourvèdre-based red wine
that is bold and dark.

Unlike the opening ceremonies, the tent for the grand tasting only had three sides so attendees could wander in and out of the open side and stand at round high top tables on a small section of fenced-in lawn. Two guitar players played on a stage in the corner, their acoustic covers of popular songs filling the area.

I wore a high-collared blouse, along with a few brushes of foundation, to hide the bruises on my neck, and my purple Certified pin adorned the lapel of my jacket. If all went well with the test in two days, it might be one of the last times I would wear it. I hadn't studied as much as I should have over the weekend, but I definitely practiced blind tasting under pressure.

"Ms. Stillwell, I'm glad you could make it

today," said Mr. Tinsley as he stood at the opening to the fence and the only way to get into the tent. He had been briefed on the situation by Dean and knew about the attack.

"Yes, I'm here and ready." I also knew that local law enforcement were waiting with Dean outside the New Sierra, per Mr. Tinsley's request, to take Isabella in for questioning once the festival was over. There still wasn't any proof she had done anything wrong and the Lancaster lacked hallway cameras to catch evidence of the assault.

"Perfect," said Mr. Tinsley. "Your position is at the sparkling and white wine section."

I went to the center of the tent, where tables formed a large empty square so attendees could walk around the outside and see the selection of wines while the pourers stood inside.

Darius, a member of my tasting group and a fellow Trentino employee, gave me a nod as he entered the tent.

"You made it," I said as he arrived at the pouring station and took his place next to me.

"Yeah, drove down this morning." He looked around. "I have tomorrow off so I'm gonna visit friends. You?"

"I have the whole week off. Flying to

Arizona."

"That's right, the test. Good luck with that."

"Thanks. I'll need it."

The partition was released and the crowd flowed into the tent. It would be the biggest event of the weekend, with many locals and visitors purchasing a single-day pass.

We quickly went through a bottle of the sparkling Rosé and I opened a new one, twisting the cork off without a sound.

"Oh, it's flat," said the attendee in front of me. "There was no pop."

"It's not flat, it's just a trick to open it. It also keeps the wine from fizzing up and spilling."

She raised her eyebrows and stared at me, clearly still skeptical.

"Here, give me your glass. You'll see."

She held it out and I poured the wine. "There's bubbles!" she exclaimed. "So wait, how did you do that?"

"You twist the cork as you're opening it. It keeps the sound to a whisper, but it takes a lot of practice, or at least it did for me." It was part of the Certified Sommelier Exam, to open the bottle without a sound.

She nodded, her glass already empty. She moved it toward me.

"Okay, which one would you like to try now?"

"That Champagne." She pointed to a bottle from Napa.

I poured it into her glass. "This is Napa Sparkling Wine made from all white grapes."

"Thanks," she said as she took a sip. "I just love Champagne."

I was about to explain what classifies Champagne, but she was already gone, either off to get food or to meet her friends.

"My favorite wine buddy," said Walt as he stepped toward the table and held out his glass. "I believe we have a previous arrangement."

"Which wine would you like?" I motioned to the bottles in front of me.

"All of them," replied Walt.

I picked up one from the tub of ice. "This is the 2015 Pinot Gris from Oregon with flavors of peach and lemon," I said as I poured him an ounce.

He looked at the level of the wine and back at me. "I don't think that was part of our deal, buddy."

"I won the blind tasting fair and square but keep coming back and I'll give you more wine. However" — I paused as I took the same bottle and added an additional ounce to his glass — "there you go."

Ben stepped up to the table. "I'd like two pours as well please." He pointed to another bottle. "Of that one."

I poured an ounce.

"What about the second one?"

"Challenge me to a blind tasting and maybe you'll get a second pour."

"I can't do that stuff," grumbled Ben as he walked away.

I glanced around the tent. There was Isabella. She looked as nervous as ever, fidgeting with restless motions as she sat at a side table. Though I knew it was all an act. She wasn't really nervous. She was a killer and she was strong.

When the grand tasting slowed down, I was able to leave my post and wander around while Darius covered for me. Dean stood at a high top table in the corner.

"I thought you would be outside."

"I'm trying my best not to let you out of my sight. I want you to be safe."

My eyes drifted to the small plates of food that covered his table. "What's this?" All of them were untouched.

"Nearly every dish they're serving at the booths. I figured you wouldn't have a chance to get around to all of them during your break, so I did it for you."

"You're adorable."

"I try. Sorry some of them are cold."

"Thanks." I picked up the first plate but kept an eye on Isabella. "I should have done something last night."

"What could you have done?"

"I don't know, but what if she leaves? She knows we're onto her. That's why she attacked me."

"She's still here. The officers will take her in for questioning after the event."

"And charge her with nothing. I'm guessing she'll leave after Hudson's announcement." I finished a tempura shrimp and tried a braised beef taco. When I looked again, Isabella was no longer at her table. "Where did she go?"

Dean looked over my shoulder. "On the far side of the tent with Walt and Ben."

"Perfect." I wiped my hands on a napkin. "I'm going to go say hi."

"Katie . . ."

"What? I'll be safe." I shined my imaginary halo. "You can come."

Dean gave me a stern look. "Don't leave the tent."

I pointed to my pin. "I won't. I'm working."

Dean stayed at the table as I approached Isabella, Walt, and Ben. My lungs constricted and I tried to take a deep breath, but the tightness remained. I had no idea what I was going to say and the bruises on my neck almost seemed to radiate pain as I got closer.

"Hey, guys."

"Hey," said Walt and Ben in unison.

"Aren't you supposed to be pouring? I don't think I'm done drinking," added Walt.

"Just on a quick break." I glanced at the three of them as an idea came to my mind. Maybe I could get Isabella to do something that would incriminate her. "So you guys, this is on the DL, but I heard they're about to arrest someone for the murder of Rachel Carlson."

Isabella jumped and Ben shuddered.

"Wait, who is Rachel Carlson?" asked Walt.

"The festival attendee who was murdered."

"I thought her name was Jocelyn," said Ben.

"No, it was always Rachel Carlson. She stole Jocelyn Rivers's badge."

"I hate all this talk about murder," said Isabella. "How can people be so evil?"

I stared at her. "I totally agree."

"So Jocelyn Rivers was Rachel Carlson," said Ben. "Rachel Carlson was Jocelyn Rivers. Jocelyn Rivers —"

"We get it, Ben," interrupted Walt.

"Yeah," I continued. "They found the evidence they needed and they're going to make an arrest."

Isabella rubbed her arms. "Can we talk about something else? This subject gives me the heebie-jeebies."

"What did I miss?" asked Anita as she joined the group.

"They're about to arrest someone for the murder of Rachel Carlson," said Walt.

"Who is also Jocelyn Rivers," added Ben.

"Are they arresting Hudson?" asked Anita.

"I'm not sure." I shrugged. "So, what's everyone drinking?"

"Wine," Walt and Ben replied in unison.

"I have Cabernet Franc," said Anita as she moved back and forth to the music. "Actually, let me be more cool when I say it." She held up her glass. "A Cab Franc."

"I want one of those," said Ben.

"You still won't be able to dance," replied Walt.

Isabella continued to rub her arms.

I glanced at my watch, even though time wasn't an issue for me. "Oops, I have to get back to my station. Let me know if you want another drink." I stepped away and left the four of them to talk. Hopefully the seed I planted was enough for Isabella to make a mistake.

I stopped by Dean's table. "Keep an eye on her and Hudson."

"What did you do?"

I shrugged. "I said an arrest was imminent. If I were her, I'd ditch the evidence or something."

"Katie," said Dean.

"I know, but it might work," I replied.

"Thank you again for coming to the Harvest Days Wine and Food Festival," said Hudson from the middle of the tent, a microphone in his hand.

"Gotta go," I whispered to Dean. "It's show time."

I returned to the pouring station as Hudson continued. "It's been a fantastic weekend, don't you agree?"

The crowd roared in approval.

"We only have a few more hours left, so make sure to enjoy every minute. I also wanted to add," he said as he glanced around the tent and paused awkwardly when his gaze landed on Isabella, "that I'm pleased to add a partnership with Tama Winery to my ever-growing resume." He raised his glass of red wine. "So let's all eat, drink, and be merry!"

The crowd cheered and activity resumed

in the tent.

I looked at Dean and nodded. He headed to the exit, most likely to meet up with the officers on the lawn.

"There's only a few more days till your test," said Darius.

"Yep."

"Are you studying while you're here?"

"Not as much as I would like. I have that flash card app on my phone."

"Which one? I want to see if it's different from mine."

I handed him my phone as I watched Walt, Ben, Anita, and Isabella on the far side of the tent. Walt and Ben moved to a line at a food booth, but Isabella stood near Anita as she continued dancing.

"I'd like to try that one," said a guest, pointing to a bottle of Viognier.

"Of course." I poured an ounce into the glass and looked back at the group across the tent. Anita was still there, but Isabella had disappeared. I glanced around for Hudson. He was gone, too.

THIRTY-FOUR:
PAIRING SUGGESTION: PETIT VERDOT — NAPA VALLEY, CALIFORNIA

A thick-skinned grape primarily used for blending, but also produced as a single varietal.

I looked around the tent in case Isabella had moved to a table or went to get more food, but I couldn't see her. The officers expected Isabella to leave through the main exit by the New Sierra so they would catch her on the way out and ask her questions, but the seam of the tent was pulled open near where she had been standing. Unless the officers had surrounded the entire area — and I was pretty certain they hadn't gone to that extreme since there was still no proof she had done anything — they would miss her. My other concern was Hudson. Was she following him somewhere? Now that the announcement was done, would she kill him, too?

"Darius, can you cover for me again?"

"What about my break?"

"Sorry, I'll be back as soon as I can."

Darius pointed at me. "I'm not getting paid for this and now I don't even get a chance to look at the food options? You owe me."

"Yes, yes, a bottle of Oban. I know," I replied, referencing his favorite Scotch and one I had bought him before when he covered shifts for me at Trentino.

A sly grin spread across his face. "Cool. Now hurry up, so at least I can eat."

I crossed the tent, dodging people as I walked, and made it through the open seam. Isabella was nearly to the entrance of the Lancaster. Her room was at the New Sierra, so she was either leaving or following Hudson. I looked behind me but saw only festival goers nearby. There wasn't time to get Dean or the officers near the New Sierra. She would be out of sight within seconds. I followed her, staying far enough behind to not look suspicious.

Isabella entered the hotel, stopped at the front desk for a moment, and looked around. I tried to duck behind a potted plant but ended up smacking my leg on the coffee table by the lobby couches.

I dropped to the floor behind a couch and rubbed my shin, hoping that she didn't see me as I tried to smooth out the pain. I reached for my pocket to text Dean what was happening but came up empty. My phone was back with Darius at the event. I peeked my head over the top of the couch. I could just see the back of Isabella's brown curls as she entered the elevator. I stood up and avoided the coffee table as I scurried across the lobby. I knew I was drawing attention to myself and people were looking, but I didn't want to lose her.

I grabbed a pen at the front desk and flipped over a flyer for their weekly activities. "I need you to call John Dean at this number and tell him that Katie said Isabella is here at the Lancaster."

I glanced back at the elevator to see what floor it stopped at. The lever above the elevator pointed to three. "Third floor."

"I don't think I can do that," said the front desk attendant. "But there's a house phone over there." She pointed across the lobby. I took one step but saw the elevator was on its way back down.

"I don't have time, please do this for me. Detective John Dean." I pushed the paper toward her and jogged to the elevator. The ride seemed to take longer than usual. When the car stopped on the third floor, I cautiously stepped into the hallway. Isabella wasn't outside Hudson's new room nor was she anywhere in sight. Maybe I had seen the wrong number on the outside of the elevator.

I continued until the hallway turned. She wasn't in that section, either.

"Katie," said a voice from behind. I turned and there was Isabella, looking as sweet and innocent as ever.

"Oh, hi, Isabella."

"Are you following me?" She still sounded nervous, but there seemed to be an edge to her voice. I worried she might attack me again and I mentally kicked myself for leaving my phone with Darius.

"No, not at all. I'm just heading to my room."

"Me, too."

"Funny, I didn't think you had a room here," I added.

Her face shifted into concern. "Is it against the rules not to stay at the main festival hotel?"

"You mentioned the other day that you were staying at the New Sierra, that's all."

Isabella jumped like she was frightened, though I knew it was an act. "Must have made a mistake."

"Are you checking out?"

"Me? No. I just want to grab my sweater

and get back to the festival. Are you done working?"

"No," I replied. "Heading back any minute." I wasn't sure what else to do. I didn't buy her sweater comment and I was certain she was about to flee. I glanced at the elevator. Did the desk clerk call Dean? I hoped he would arrive soon.

She opened the door to her room. "You can come in while I look for my sweater. Then we'll head back together."

I was worried she might attack me again, but I also didn't want to let her out of my sight.

I moved inside, but kept the door open with my foot in case I needed to make a fast exit.

"I'm glad you decided to wait with me," she said as she searched through her suitcase. "It makes sense since you were following me."

"I actually wasn't, but you sound a little guilty there. Have something to hide?" My voice came out strong, even though my nerves were rampant.

"I think it's perfectly reasonable to ask why someone's following me. Don't you?"

"If I was indeed following you, which I wasn't." I smiled.

"This is silly," said Isabella.

"I agree. But you should know I know about Rachel."

Isabella tilted her head. "What do you mean?" she said in a high, sweet voice.

"That you paid her to get close to Hudson. I don't understand why you didn't just approach him yourself."

She turned her attention to the open suitcase in front of her. "This conversation would be much more engaging if I actually knew what you were talking about."

"The police are outside. They're going to take you in for questioning."

"On what grounds? I've done nothing wrong." She smiled at me. "Life is complicated, Katie. Don't complicate it further by doing whatever it is you are doing now."

"You killed Rachel Carlson."

Isabella pulled her sweater out, looked at me, and smiled. "Katie, you don't know what you're talking about. I suggest you go off and play with your boyfriend and leave wine things to those of us who know what we're doing." She walked toward me and I flinched, but she simply entered the bathroom and riffled through her makeup bag.

"He's already on his way here with the authorities."

Isabella paused. "You're joking."

"Am I? I don't think so."

She laughed and applied her lipstick with a steady hand.

I stood at the door, not sure what to do next, but then I saw it. At the edge of the open suitcase was a flash of bright blue. Like the hat the bartender mentioned. Without thinking, I stepped toward the suitcase to get a closer look and heard the door close behind me.

I turned around to reopen it, but there was Isabella with a large kitchen knife. "Silly Katie." She pointed the knife toward me. "You should have left when you had the chance. I tried to warn you, but you kept asking questions. Kept pushing." All nervousness was gone from her voice, the act finally dropped. Now she sounded more like my attacker in the hallway.

"It doesn't have to be like this, Isabella. We can talk about it." The tip of the knife was only three feet away. It was better than having a gun aimed at me, but still not exactly comforting.

"No." Isabella held the knife with her hand over the top of the handle. It would be difficult to stab me that way, but I wasn't about to point it out. "You shouldn't be here," she said.

"Clearly," I responded. "But it's a little too late for that." The only thing I had close to a weapon was the small blade on my wine opener. It would be no match for the large knife she was brandishing. "I know you paid Rachel, but how did you know her?"

"I found her at a gym in Santa Barbara. She was eager to earn a few dollars so I hired her to convince Hudson to join Tama Winery. By whatever means necessary. That doesn't mean I'm a killer."

"But she failed, didn't she?"

"I don't know what you're talking about." She smiled sweetly as she waved the knife. "Hudson announced that he's with Tama Winery now."

"Hudson didn't want to join. At least until you locked him in the closet in the restaurant. Then he was eager to be a part of your little company. What did you do, blackmail him?"

Isabella laughed. "Blackmail? Don't be ridiculous. I simply gave Hudson a little time to think things over. I wasn't going to leave him in there, but I got distracted. I mean, it's a festival after all." A wicked smile formed on her face. "How did you know it was me? I left no evidence."

"But you did. The wine bottle in Rachel's hand."

"What does that matter?"

"You were the only one who knew it was

Tama wine last night. It was in a different bottle. It meant you were connected."

"That's entrapment."

"Why? I'm not law enforcement."

"It's not enough to convict me."

"No, it's not. But we do have this." I motioned to the space between us.

"Self-defense," said Isabella. "I'm a sweetheart. They'll believe me."

"Hardly."

Her eyes narrowed and her smile disappeared. "I should have put you outside Hudson's door instead of Rachel."

I felt a chill climb the back of my neck. "Thanks for the sentiment."

Isabella swung the knife in my direction, but I jumped, the bed hitting my calves.

She laughed as she swiped once more. "I'll never hire someone to help me again. What a mess! I should have done the whole thing by myself from the start."

"Why didn't you?" I tried to think how I could grab the knife, but her movements were rapid and jerky. If I did anything, it would just end up cutting me.

She jabbed the knife toward me and I dodged to the right. "I was a silent partner. I didn't want my name out there. I've put my entire life savings into Tama. It has to succeed. All Rachel did was try to follow

Hudson for other reasons. She had her own agenda." Isabella shook her head. "She was ridiculous from the beginning. Stealing someone else's pass when I gave her enough money to buy her own? That's just greedy."

"So that's why you killed her?"

Isabella shrugged. "I snapped, what can I say? It wasn't like I planned to kill her." She tossed her hair back and the pause was enough for me to jump behind the bed and pull my wine opener from my pocket. It wasn't much, but it would have to do.

"You think that's any match against this knife?" She laughed. "Please. You're even dumber than I thought."

"Just trying to even up the playing field. In fact, if you put your knife down, I'll put this one down, too." My nerves were actually calm and I could breathe. It was like I had been prepared for this situation, though I had no idea how.

"Not a chance."

"Okay then. The status quo remains." I held my opener up, keeping the space of the mattress between us. If she came around it, I could go over the top. If she jumped up on the bed, I could try and get around the side, but I wasn't sure I would make it in time. I needed to figure something out before she lunged again. "Not to point out the obvious, but my boyfriend is a detective. He'll know that you're the one who killed me and Rachel and tied up Hudson."

"This is self-defense, Katie. You followed me and attacked me with that little opener. What makes you think I can't get away with it?" She reached over the bed so fast, the knife made a whooshing sound as I threw myself to the side. It missed me.

"You didn't get away with Rachel's murder," I said as I scrambled to my feet.

"Oh, but I did, and I'm about to take care of you."

"They'll be here soon. The police."

"This room isn't even under my name. The one at the New Sierra is. I'm telling you, Katie, I know how to cover my tracks and you can't jump into the bushes this time." She smiled and I knew she was the one that tried to run me off the road.

Adrenaline pulsed through my veins. "They'll still link it to you. You're already wanted for questioning. You couldn't have covered everything."

"I'll have to take the risk," said Isabella as she jumped onto the bed and swiped the knife at me. I tried to move to the side again, but she was too close. The tip of her knife sliced through my shirt.

I grabbed at my stomach as she retreated,

a strange smile on her face. I looked down at the line of blood forming on the fabric, though I felt no pain. "Seriously?"

"All part of the game, Katie. I have a knife and you have a silly little wine opener." She grinned. "Just means I'm more prepared than you."

"Is this what you did to Rachel? Stab her in front of Hudson's door and leave her there as a warning to him?" I held my abdomen with one hand while I kept the wine opener up with the other. At least the shock was keeping away the pain, but I knew I was in trouble. I was cornered and wounded.

Isabella stood on the bed, staring at me as she held her knife. I moved alongside the bed until I was in the middle of the room, but my movements didn't seem to faze her.

"It wasn't supposed to be that way. Rachel was supposed to bring him to me. This room, in fact. One conversation and he would have done what I wanted. But she failed. When I caught her in the hallway and she said she was leaving, I snapped." She shrugged. "It happens to the best of us. I had to think quick, so I left her there."

"You're lying." I took a step backward to the door. "People would have heard."

"You'd be surprised at what people ignore

when it's late at night and they're tucked safely in their beds." She paused. "Or busy at a grand tasting." She lunged toward me, her knife high in the air.

I threw my arm up to block her attack as she landed. My forearm hit hers and sent it to the side as I grabbed her hand, twisting it around and barely missing the blade.

She punched with her other hand, smacking me in the face. I pulled both hands behind her back, my knee in the middle of her spine as I took her down to the ground, the knife clattering to the floor.

"Wow," said a male voice.

I glanced up as Isabella struggled underneath me. A hotel employee held a ring of keys at the door with Dean, who pushed past him. "We came just in time."

"How did you know where to find me?" I released my grasp on Isabella as he handcuffed her.

"I got your message from the front desk. We've been opening nearly every door on the third floor." Dean's face went pale. "Katie, you're hurt."

I put my hand over my abdomen to try and stop the bleeding. "I'm fine. I think. But I had her, so what did you mean about coming just in time?"

"To see those moves. Where did you learn those?"

"I don't know. Maybe the Academy. Maybe karate class when I was a kid."

"I'm impressed," said Dean. "What other tricks are you hiding?"

"Do you have to talk about this right now?" said Isabella. "I want to press charges."

"Sorry, I don't think that's an option," replied Dean. "Come on, let's go. I have some boys in blue who want to meet you." He glanced at me. "And we need to get you to a doctor."

"Take care of Isabella first. I want to see her in the back of a squad car, knowing that she's fully trapped. Then we can worry about this." I took a good look at my stomach for the first time. The cut was deeper than I had realized.

THIRTY-FIVE:
PAIRING SUGGESTION:
TOKAJI ASZÚ —
TOKAJ, HUNGARY

Created from grapes affected by
botrytis (Noble Rot), this wine is
golden and sweet.

The police officers put Isabella in the back of the car as medics tended to my injury. A crowd had formed to watch the squad cars and ambulance arrive, but the temptation of food and wine won in the end and now only a small group remained focused on the activity.

"You'll need stitches, but I've secured it with bandages for the moment," said the medic.

The pain had set in once the shock wore off, but I didn't want to show it in my face. "Great, just what I need. A lovely scar."

"Scars can be cool," said the medic. "Besides, you're lucky it wasn't worse. Do you want to come in the ambulance?"

I shook my head. "We'll drive in our own

car. I don't need all of the flashing lights."

The medic stared at me, a skeptical look on his face.

"Don't worry, I'm going to go to the hospital," I added. "Save the ambulance for those who really need it."

"I'll drive her," said Dean.

I looked up at him. "Not exactly a great end to our special weekend."

"I wouldn't say that. Wine, food, and stitches." Dean touched my shoulder. "I'm just glad you're okay.

One of the officers came over to Dean, holding a pair of handcuffs. "I think these are yours."

"They are."

"Okay, then. Thanks for your help today," said the officer. "We're going to take her in now. We'll need your statement. Both of you."

"Definitely," replied Dean.

The officer glanced at me. I wanted to point to my bandages and tell him that he would get the statement after I had stitches because I had been in a knife fight, but I decided to let it go. "Not a problem," I replied.

"Come over when you're ready," the officer said and walked away.

I looked at Dean. "You always carry

handcuffs on you?"

"Force of habit." Dean didn't smile. "Will you be okay for Tuesday?"

"Of course. But at the moment, don't remind me." I put my hand on my stomach, the bandages awkward and bulky with a tremor of pain beneath them.

Hudson ambled over from the officers, the ever-present wineglass in his hand. "Katie, Dean, thank you for everything. I really appreciate it." He motioned to the bandages around my waist. "Is that from Isabella?"

"Yeah. She had a bigger knife, but I won in the end."

"Are you okay?"

"I will be after a few stitches, but Hudson, I still don't understand why you didn't tell the police after Isabella kidnapped you."

Hudson shook his head. "Isabella knew where I lived and knew my wife and kids were there without me. She said if I didn't go along with it or if I involved the police, she had an associate waiting near my house." He shrugged. "I figured it wasn't worth the risk. I mean, it's just a winery. I can promote that if it means the safety of my family."

"Are they safe now?"

He nodded. "Officers are at the house and apparently Isabella's now backpedaling, saying there wasn't even anyone waiting. I also heard from the owners of Tama a few minutes ago. They had no idea she was doing this. Looks like I have some legal issues to deal with this week but no matter what, I'll be at the exam." He paused as he looked at us. "I don't know what I would have done if you weren't here. Either I'd be in jail or I'd be . . ." His voice fell away before he could finish his sentence. He took a sip of his wine. "Anyway, thank you." He motioned to my bandages. "I guess this means you won't be there on Tuesday."

"Are you kidding? I'm not letting this hold me back. I'll be in Phoenix."

"Good to hear," said Hudson as he nodded. "Unfortunately your work this weekend won't affect the test results."

"I would be upset if it did," I replied. "I want to be judged on my wine knowledge, not my ability to solve crimes or end up in knife fights."

"I'll see you on Tuesday then." He glanced at Dean. "Or at least one of you. Are you taking the exam?"

"No. I'm not a sommelier. I'm a detective," replied Dean.

"Ah, that makes sense then. You did a lot of good detecting this weekend."

"Actually, it was mostly Katie. She's excel-

303

lent at it."

Hudson looked at me. "I hope this doesn't mean you're leaving the wine world."

I smiled. "Not a chance."

Hudson nodded. "I should get back to the tent. But thank you again. See you in a few days."

Dean turned to me once Hudson had walked away. "You know, you are really good at this. You might want to consider a career shift."

"I don't know. I like helping people learn about wine and choosing the right one for their meal as I share the story of each bottle. I love wine too much to step away from it."

"You could do both. You could be a wine detective."

"Is there even such a thing?"

"There could be." Dean smiled. "You could investigate wine crimes."

"You sound like my dad."

"I'm sure he would love it."

I laughed but groaned as it caused the pain to increase. "But I'm not doing the Police Academy again."

"Just saying, there might be a future in it. And you wouldn't have to do the Academy. You could be a private investigator. We could even team up."

"That would be nice to work together. We

make a pretty good team."

"Yes, we do. After your test this week, you'll have some free time." Dean nodded. "While still studying for the Master Sommelier Exam," he quickly added.

Mr. Tinsley cleared his throat. I hadn't even noticed him approach, but he now stood only a few feet away. "Ms. Stillwell, I can't tell you how much we've enjoyed having you here this weekend. We'll soon be in the planning stages for next year, but I already know that we'd love to have you host some panels. What do you think?"

Dean winked at me and I smiled. "That would be great."

"Wonderful," said Mr. Tinsley. "We'll be in touch." He turned to Dean. "Mr. Stillwell, thank you for your help this weekend. I appreciated your efforts to keep the police activity from deterring from the festival."

"It was my pleasure." Dean paused. "Actually, my last name's not Stillwell."

Mr. Tinsley's face fell.

"It's okay. In a way it was nice because I was so closely associated with Katie."

"If you're rejoining us at the grand tasting, I'll get you a new name badge. The correct one this time."

"Thanks, but I think we have a hospital visit ahead."

"Of course." Mr. Tinsley glanced at my abdomen. "I hope you'll be okay."

"I'll be fine."

"Thank you again." Mr. Tinsley walked away.

"See," said Dean. "I told you there would be more seminars in your future."

"Let's just hope no more murders," I replied as I looked at the lawn and the activity around it. The hum of the festival had returned. "Overall, it was a good weekend. I was able to put a murderer behind bars, free an innocent man from suspicion, and practice blind tasting. And I'll still get some studying in before the weekend is over." I took out my phone. Darius had returned it when I was with the medic. "In fact, is it okay if I study while you drive us back to San Francisco?"

"Definitely, but hospital first."

"Don't remind me."

THIRTY-SIX:
PAIRING SUGGESTION:
LATE HARVEST RIESLING —
COLUMBIA VALLEY,
WASHINGTON

A sweet wine made from grapes gathered after harvest, because some things are worth the wait.

The Phoenix, Arizona, weather was warm, but I still felt a chill as Dean and I stood outside the hotel where my exam would take place. It was Tuesday, just two days after the knife fight with Isabella, and the healing had barely started.

"Do you feel okay?" asked Dean.

I nodded. "I mean, sure. It's only my career on the line."

"You can take the test again if you don't pass, but I believe in you," said Dean. "However, I was asking about your laceration. Has it healed enough to carry a tray?"

"It'll be fine." I touched my stomach, the bandage hidden under my suit. "I mean, it only hurts a little bit, I just hope I don't pop any stitches during the exam."

"What will you do if that happens?"

I looked at Dean. "Just keep going."

"Rock star." He smiled. "Quick, what's the river in Portugal that goes through the wine regions?"

"You mean the Douro River?" I laughed. "Look at you, throwing out trivia without even having flash cards in your hand."

"I've learned some things along the way."

A car parked near us and two guys in suits adorned with purple Certified Sommelier pins exited and walked toward the hotel.

"Do you want to go check in?"

"You mean, am I ready for the start of a three-day examination that tests everything I know about wine and has a very low pass rate?"

"That, too."

I took a breath, but I could feel the tightness in my lungs. "I hope so. I've worked hard for this." But I didn't move. I wasn't ready to enter. Not yet.

"You can't stay out here forever," said Dean, as if reading my mind.

"I know. I'm excited, but . . ." I paused. My lungs wouldn't expand. I decided to ignore it, though it was easier said than done. "It's going to be good." I stared at the entrance to the hotel. "I guess this is it."

"Good luck. I'll be waiting here for you

on Thursday."

"You don't have to wait. I can call you when I'm done."

"No way. I want to be here for you the minute it's over. No matter the outcome. I won't move from this spot. Just ignore the fact that I have a hotel booked up the road."

I smiled. "You aren't even supposed to be here. You should be working on the Harper case."

"After your injury, I wanted to make sure you made it today. This is worth the personal days."

"Thank you." I glanced at the building. "You can come inside with me, you know. You don't have to avoid the whole hotel. You just can't come into the exam portions."

"I don't want to be a distraction. Besides, you can hang out with the other somms. Quiz each other. Laugh. All that good stuff. I'll be waiting for you in this very spot when the test is done."

"Stop." I laughed, but then looked into his eyes and smiled. "But seriously, thank you."

He leaned over and kissed me. "Now go get 'em, The Palate."

I saluted and turned toward the hotel. When I reached the front door, I glanced back at Dean. He hadn't moved and pointed to his feet to prove it.

I smiled and walked through the revolving door. This was it. Ready or not, it was time to take my Advanced Exam, the next step in my goal to become a Master Sommelier. Just over two hundred people around the world held the title and only a small percentage of them were women. But I was going to become one of them. I wasn't going to let work, murders, or knife fight injuries stop me.

I was on my way.

ABOUT THE AUTHOR

Nadine Nettmann, a Certified Sommelier through the Court of Master Sommeliers, is always on the lookout for great wines and the stories behind them. She has visited wine regions around the world including Chile, South Africa, Spain, Germany, and every region in France. Nadine is a member of Mystery Writers of America, Sisters in Crime, and International Thriller Writers. She lives in California with her husband.

The employees of Thorndike Press hope you have enjoyed this Large Print book. All our Thorndike, Wheeler, and Kennebec Large Print titles are designed for easy reading, and all our books are made to last. Other Thorndike Press Large Print books are available at your library, through selected bookstores, or directly from us.

For information about titles, please call:
  (800) 223-1244

or visit our website at:
  gale.com/thorndike

To share your comments, please write:
  Publisher
  Thorndike Press
  10 Water St., Suite 310
  Waterville, ME 04901